Ginger pushed Todd's wheelchair slowly up the steep path. Even if they didn't get very far, it'd be worth it for Todd to see as much as he could and to take pictures.

"You can stop here now," Todd said. "I want to get those trees in the picture."

Ginger stopped, and he snapped a picture, then another.

"Okay."

The trail grew steeper and steeper, with rocks and roots sticking out here and there. Ginger pushed the wheelchair onward, not seeing the rock at the edge of the path. Suddenly a wheel bumped over it.

"Yii!" she cried out, struggling with the wheelchair.

Todd yelled, "Hold it!"

She held on with all of her might. "I can't!"

Todd and the wheelchair tipped sideways over the edge, sliding down the forested hillside while she ran after it!

"Help!" she shouted. "Someone, help!"

The Ginger Series
by Elaine L. Schulte

Here Comes Ginger!
Off to a New Start
A Job for an Angel
Absolutely Green
Go For It!

GO FOR IT!

Elaine L. Schulte

Chariot Books™
David C. Cook Publishing Co.

A White Horse Book
Published by Chariot Books™,
an imprint of David C. Cook Publishing Co.
David C. Cook Publishing Co., Elgin, Illinois 60120
David C. Cook Publishing Co., Weston, Ontario
Nova Distribution LTD., Torquay, England

GO FOR IT!
© 1991 by Elaine L. Schulte

With special appreciation for assistance to Dr. Ronald
Creque, Pastor, Yosemite Community Church, and to
Dave Kelley, Director of Summit Adventure.

Cover design by AD/Plus, Ltd.
Cover illustration by Janice Skivington
First printing, 1991
Printed in the United States of America
95 94   2 3 4 5

Library of Congress Cataloging-in-Publication Data

Schulte, Elaine L.
    Go for it! / Elaine Schulte
        p.   cm.—(A White horse book)
    Summary: Apprehensive about going with Grandfather
Gabriel to stay with stepcousins in Yosemite, Ginger finds
them all friendly and welcoming except for fifteen-year-old
Todd who is paralyzed and confined to a wheelchair.
    ISBN 1-55513-384-3
    [1. Cousins—Fiction. 2. Interpersonal relations—Fiction.
3. Camping—Fiction. 4. Christian life—Fiction. 5. Yosemite
National Park (Calif.)—Fiction.] I. Title.
PZ7.S3867Go   1991
[Fic]—dc 20   91-8615
                                                        CIP
                                                        AC

*To all of those who, in their own way,
trust and "Go for It!"*

1

Chewing her gum hard, Ginger peered into her suitcase. Jeans, sweatshirts, shorts, T-shirts, socks, new summer dress. It looked like she had everything she needed for her trip with Grandfather Gabriel to Yosemite. There was even a tag with her name on it dangling from the suitcase handle: *Ginger Anne Trumbell*, it read.

"You'll have a wonderful time," her mother assured her as she stepped into Ginger's bedroom.

"I hope so," Ginger answered.

She felt excited about going, but a little strange, too. They would stay with Grandfather's relatives—actually her stepaunt, stepuncle, and stepcousins—none of whom she knew.

"Of course you'll have a wonderful time," Mom said again. She wore her blue robe and held two-week-old Mattie over her shoulder, patting his back. With his tiny fingers tangled in her wavy auburn hair, he looked precious. Then he gave a loud, obnoxious b-u-r-p.

"Good job," Mom told him and then laughed with Ginger.

"I can't believe you burped me like that!"

Mom laughed again. "I expect almost every person on earth has at one time been burped."

"I guess so."

Seeing Mom look so cozy with Mattie, Ginger felt even less like going to Yosemite. "I don't know, Mom—"

"We'll manage," her mother promised, her dimples deepening. "Besides, you've worked hard helping with Mattie. You could stand a rest. Gram just called, too, and she's on her way now to help with washing and cooking. We'd all feel good about your having at least a little vacation this summer. This hasn't been the easist year for you."

"I guess not." So much had happened, it boggled Ginger's mind to think of all of it.

A year ago she'd been desperately trying to stop Mom's romance with Grant Gabriel. Then, a week before the wedding, she'd amazingly become a Christian. And a week after the wedding, in which she'd been a junior bridesmaid, she'd moved into the Gabriel house with Grant and his family: Lilabet, who was four now; Joshua, who was twelve; and Grandfather Gabriel, who lived out in the guest house behind the pool.

As if that weren't enough, she'd transferred to a Christian school and had a brand-new baby brother. Being part of a "blended family" wasn't always easy, but it was interesting!

Mom said, "Don't forget your new white sandals for your special dinner with Grandfather at the Ahwahnee Hotel."

"Uff, I almost forgot!" Ginger headed for the closet. She grabbed them from the mess on the closet floor and stuffed them under her jeans in the suitcase. "Ready," she said. "I guess I'll go."

"I'm glad, Ginger, because Grandfather is getting a bit absentminded about taking his heart pills."

"You want *me* to watch if he takes his pills?"

Mom nodded. "It would make us feel more comfortable."

It didn't make Ginger feel too comfortable.

"You're going to have a wonderful time, Ginger," her mother said for the third time.

"I hope so," she answered. "I sure do hope so."

Half an hour later, after breakfast, Ginger waved out the car window at her family. "Goodbye!" she yelled. "Goodbye, all!"

" 'Bye, Ginger! 'Bye, Grandfather!" they called back.

As they drove down the driveway, Grandfather Gabriel said happily, "We're off to Yosemite!"

"Yeah," Ginger answered, "we're off to Yosemite." She tried to sound pleased about it and chewed her gum fast.

9

She glanced back at her family. They stood outside the old white Spanish house in the early morning sunshine; they looked like a picture framed by purple bougainvillea blooming near the rooftop and red geraniums surrounding the lawn.

Mom was still in her blue robe, holding Mattie against her shoulder. Grant stood behind them, waving and looking like a proud new father. Lilabet clutched her yellow blanket and waved wildly. And Raffles, their old hairy English sheepdog, stood with them, wagging his tail-less rear end. Only she and Grandfather and stepbrother Joshua, who was at camp, were missing from the picture.

Now that Grandfather's white Plymouth had turned onto the street and the rest of her family was out of sight, Ginger blinked as hard as she could to keep from bawling and gave her gum a loud crack.

"Goodbye to Santa Rosita Hills for a week," Grandfather said companionably.

"Yeah, goodbye to Santa Rosita Hills," she echoed to keep him company.

The neighborhood felt familiar now that she'd lived in the Gabriel house for a whole school year. One thing she really liked about her new home was the sunshine. In June it was usually foggy at the beach, where she'd lived with Mom and Dad most of her life. After their divorce, she'd lived in the little beach house alone with Mom for three years.

"Excited?" Grandfather Gabriel asked as they drove on through the neighborhood.

"A little." She darted a glance at him and felt better already. His silvery hair glinted in the sunshine, and his lips curved up with enthusiasm, as usual.

He asked, "Do you remember Aunt Jennie and Uncle Charlie from your mother and Grant's wedding?"

"Not really," Ginger admitted. "There were too many people around."

Her stepcousins hadn't come to the wedding, but Grant had shown her a snapshot of them. Twelve-year-old Berkeley looked tall, blonde, and beautiful—not friendly or fun. And fifteen-year-old Todd was a paraplegic, stuck in a wheelchair.

"I won't know what to say to a boy like Todd," Ginger worried aloud.

"You'll do fine," Grandfather assured her.

Maybe, Ginger thought. One hopeful thing about Todd was his being at Yosemite for a special mountain-climbing expedition for handicapped people. She'd seen a video of it, and some of them were blind or in wheelchairs like Todd. Some of them didn't want to be called handicapped, either, just disabled. Or was it the other way around? She'd never been around any handicapped-disabled people. Maybe she'd say something dumb, dumb, dumb!

On top of that, Todd and Berkeley were home-schooled, and were using their visit to Yosemite as a home school field trip. Probably they'd have to study all the time, and she'd be stuck going around by herself. How did she ever let herself get talked into this trip?

Grandfather asked, "Did you pack a nice dress for

11

our date at the Ahwahnee Hotel?"

"Gram made a new one for me, white with green swirls."

"Sounds just right for a beautiful redhead," he said, reaching over to muss her wild red curls.

"Ha! I looked in the mirror this morning!" she objected. She was as freckled, green-eyed, and straight-up-and-down as ever.

"Well, I think you're beautiful," Grandfather stated firmly, though he kept his eyes on the road. "And Gram Trumbell is a good grandmother to you, taking time from her seamstress work to make you clothes."

"The part about Gram sure is right," Ginger agreed.

She reminded herself that he was a retired minister and always looked for the best in everyone—not that Gram Trumbell wasn't good. Last night she'd even brought ham sandwiches, homemade brownies, and apples for the trip so they could save money.

"Didn't want you to starve on the drive up to Yosemite!" she'd said. Adding to the complications of life in their blended family, Gram was pleased about Mom's marriage to Grant Gabriel, while Gram's son—who was Ginger's real father and Mom's first husband—was put out about their happiness!

"Wish I were going to Yosemite again myself," Gram had added. "Maybe I'll go this fall with some of my friends."

Everybody seemed to love Yosemite, Ginger thought. Some kids at school had been there two or three times. She smoothed her denim skirt across her lap and tried not to feel nervous.

Once they were driving on the freeway, her mind drifted to her stepcousin. "How did Todd get to be a—a paraplegic?"

"Hasn't anyone ever told you?"

"I don't think so. Maybe Mom did say something about a car accident. . . ."

Grandfather nodded. "His mother was driving him home from guitar practice when Todd was ten. A teenager on drugs drove through a stoplight and hit them."

Ginger gulped.

Grandfather drew a regretful breath himself. "For a long time the doctors thought he wouldn't live, but they did their best, and he finally came around. Not much could be done about his spine, though. To put the matter as simply as possible, his legs and feet don't work."

"Oh." It was a dumb answer, but she couldn't think of anything else to say. At least he wanted to climb mountains, she decided. That was really amazing for someone in a wheelchair.

As they drove onto the freeway, cars and trucks zoomed all around them. A good thing their family had prayed for travel mercies at breakfast. Both Grandfather's wife and Grant's first wife had been killed in a freeway accident. "Riding in a car sure can be dangerous," she remarked.

Grandfather nodded. "The world would be a lot better off if people never forgot that."

Ginger chewed her gum fast and watched Grandfather drive. He might be absentminded about taking his pills, but he was careful about watching the traffic all around them. There, in the slow lane, was one of those driver training cars with the warning placard "Student Driver" on the roof.

Maybe she should pay more attention to driving herself, she thought. In just four years, when she'd be going on sixteen, she'd be taking driver's training in school. It wouldn't hurt to start learning. Not that she'd tell Grandfather she was watching him. He had just turned on the car radio and probably wouldn't notice anyhow.

Hours later, when they drove up the foothills to Yosemite, Ginger decided she'd watched enough driving. The creeks, forests, and mountains reminded her of a Scripture verse about nature itself proclaiming God.

Before long, they stopped at a park entrance booth that said *Yosemite National Park*. "Welcome to Yosemite," a uniformed ranger said with a nice smile. After Grandfather had paid their fee, the ranger gave them an activities newspaper, *The Yosemite Guide*. "Enjoy your visit!" he added.

As they drove on, Ginger looked at the pine forest and Grouse Creek. "It's beautiful, but I expected something different," she said, a little disappointed.

"Just wait," Grandfather answered. "It's going to be more than just beautiful. It's going to be magnificent.

Here's the Wawona Tunnel through the mountain now."

He turned on the car lights, and they drove through the longest tunnel she'd ever been in. Drivers honked horns to hear the echoes, and she guessed if Joshua were along they'd hold their breath all the way through.

At last they drove out into bright daylight, and she could only say, "Wow!"

Huge gray mountains rose up through the beautiful green valley, and a long waterfall cascaded down over the rock. "This view is probably one of the most photographed in the world," Grandfather said. He pointed out the mountain peaks as they drove into a scenic viewpoint parking lot. "El Capitán . . . Clouds' Rest . . . Half Dome . . . Sentinel Rock . . . Cathedral Rocks."

He nodded toward the long, leaping waterfall. "There's Bridalveil Falls."

"Look at the rainbows in it!" Ginger said. "I've never seen a place so—so—"

"Magnificent?" Grandfather suggested.

She nodded. "Magnificent. Except maybe the ocean."

She wasn't the only one in awe. Plenty of other people stood around the edge of the overlook, some snapping pictures as fast as their cameras could go.

"Let's get out and stretch our legs," Grandfather said.

She climbed out of the car. Magnificent was the word for this, all right. Magnificent mountains . . . a magnificent waterfall with a rainbow . . . a huge forest. . . .

"The Indians called Bridalveil Falls *Pohono,* 'puffing wind,' because of its windblown mists," Grandfather said. "It's what rangers call a free-leaping waterfall."

They just stood and looked at the mountains and the filmy waterfall and forest under the bright blue sky. Everything was so huge and overwhelming, Ginger said, "I'm glad you know your way around."

"It helps," he agreed. "I should have brought my camera, but I have plenty of Yosemite pictures packed away at home. Besides, I know Todd will be taking slides, and we can get copies."

As they walked around the edge of the scenic overlook, they read the small metal signs that gave the names of mountains and their heights.

Nearby a tourist read aloud, "Sentinel Rock rises 3,073 feet above the valley floor. Bridalveil Falls drops 620 feet from its hanging valley into the moist, rocky basin—"

Ginger thought she could stand for a long time just gazing at the view, but Grandfather said, "Let's go on. There's a lot more to see, and plenty of ways to see it. I think you'll like bicycling and rafting and horseback riding. . . . I hope you brought your bathing suit."

"Sure." She gave her gum a good crack as they headed for the car. Despite her uneasiness about staying with Grandfather's relatives, she couldn't help feeling excited now.

16

Glancing back at the awesome scenery again, she said, "I hope Todd isn't going to climb *those* mountains!"

"I'm not certain he'll be climbing at all," Grandfather said, his voice full of concern. "Aunt Jennie phoned last night, and it seems he's not so sure he wants to go on the climbing expedition after all."

Uh oh, Ginger thought. Grandfather's news made her uneasy somehow. *Uh oh!*

2

Ginger liked the looks of their old log-trimmed cabin in the forest, even from a distance. It nestled in the forest like the other cabins, but she could already see that theirs was special. "Look, the roof is notched to make room for those huge trees," she said to Grand-father as they carried their suitcases up the dusty path from the parking lot.

"Cedar trees," Grandfather said, "incense cedar. Judging by the thickness of their trunks, those two have been here a good while longer than the cabins." He pointed out other trees near the log-lined path. "As I recall, those are Ponderosa pine, and those over there are California black oak."

Ginger spied a furry animal scampering across

nearby tree roots. "And that's a squirrel!" she pointed out as a joke.

Grandfather chuckled, then a bird squawked at them raucously. "Stellar's jay. They act like they rule the valley."

Ginger spotted the noisy blue bird on a branch in a green thicket. "He sounds bossy all right."

Close by, the brown wooden cabin looked rustic and welcoming with its wooden front deck and brown-cream-and-green plaid curtains in the windows. The first door had a small step, but the second door had a wheelchair ramp—an uncomfortable reminder that she'd never been around anyone in a wheelchair. On the far side of the cabin was a parking space and a sign that said, "Handicapped Parking Only."

Grandfather set his suitcase down on the deck by the first door and knocked.

"Coming!" a girl's voice answered from inside. Seconds later, a tall, slim girl opened the door wide.

"Berkeley!" Grandfather exclaimed happily. "My, haven't you grown in the last three months!"

She looked a little shy, then smiled. "Only because I'm standing up higher than you, Grandfather!"

"You're right! Do I get a hug?"

Berkeley opened her arms and hugged him.

Holding her suitcase, Ginger chewed her gum hard as she watched the two of them from the outdoor deck. Berkeley was pretty, with blue eyes and long blondish-brown hair that curled up at her shoulders. In her white T-shirt and shorts, it was clear that she didn't have

19

one freckle on her arms or legs.

Grandfather said, "This is your cousin Ginger."

"Hi, Ginger," Berkeley said, sounding shy. "Come in."

"Hi," Ginger replied as she stepped into the rustic room. Her stepcousin might be a little shy, but it looked as though good manners came easily to Berkeley Elizabeth Adamson, which Grandfather had said was her whole name.

"Mom hiked to the market at Yosemite Village," Berkeley explained. "And Dad and Todd drove off to talk to the people at the Summit Adventure base camp."

"Todd's at the base camp?" Grandfather repeated.

"Just to look," Berkeley explained, and they eyed each other oddly for a moment.

Grandfather must have decided not to say more about it, because he just gave Berkeley a fond pat on the shoulder. "With all of this beauty outside to enjoy, we especially thank you for waiting for us at the cabin."

"I had schoolwork to do anyhow. A unit on the Indians who once lived here."

Uff, Ginger thought. Just as she suspected. Home schoolers would forever be busy with schoolwork.

"Where do we bunk?" Grandfather asked, eyeing the rustic room with Ginger.

"This half of the cabin is for the girls—Ginger, Mom, and me," Berkeley said, then opened the connecting door to the other side. "And this is the 'boys' room' for Dad, Todd, and you. Each side has a bathroom and a closet big enough to be a dressing room, too."

"Well, then," Grandfather said, looking in the other room. "It does look like the 'boys' side' . . . a lot messier. I'll get myself settled in. I see I get the bed by the back window. Expect I'll have to ward off any bears that break in."

Berkeley smiled. "We haven't seen a bear yet!"

"In that case," Grandfather said, "I'll head back out to the car to bring in our cooler of food."

When he left, Berkeley turned to Ginger. "We've given you the last bed by the window, too. We hadn't thought of bears, though. Mom thought you might not enjoy being stuck in the middle of us."

Ginger lugged her suitcase to the last bed. "I guess I could take care of a bear," she began, then realized it sounded like the old Ginger, the one who was always bragging. She added quickly, "If one comes, I'll get under the bed!"

Her stepcousin gave a surprised laugh. "Me, too! I—I hope you'll call me Berkie."

"Thanks . . . Berkie," Ginger replied, encouraged.

Berkie said, "Besides doing schoolwork, I've been scouting around for places for us to go and things to do."

"Great," Ginger replied. The week looked a little more hopeful already. Maybe things would work out yet, she decided as she plopped her suitcase on her bed. The bedspreads, she noticed, matched the plaid curtains.

Looking around the room, she saw that the walls were a grooved wood that had been painted cream, probably ages ago. Nearby stood a built-in dresser with three big drawers on the bottom and two smaller drawers on top.

"We each get one big dresser drawer," Berkie said.

"Is mine the bottom one?" Ginger guessed, thinking they'd probably taken the best already.

"No, you get the top. Mom's got the middle, and I've got the bottom so we can keep up our bending. Mom and I are sharing one of the small drawers, so you can have the little one closest to your bed. If that's all right with you."

"That's fine," Ginger said. "Guess I'll unpack now."

Berkie sat down on her bed. "There's the ledge around the room, too, but it's only wide enough for combs and hair ribbons and stuff."

"It looks like you have lots of hair ribbons," Ginger said. A row of ribbons lined the ledge above Berkie's bed, and she wore a white one on the side of her hair to match her shorts outfit.

"I collect them," Berkie said. "My hair is so straight, except at the ends, and ribbons make it look less droopy."

"Droopy?! It doesn't look droopy to me. You ought to have wild red curls like mine if you want to see trouble!"

Berkie laughed. "I wouldn't mind a few of your curls!"

Ginger smiled and started to unpack. "I brought mostly shorts and T-shirts."

"Me, too," Berkie said.

"I guess I won't change my skirt yet," Ginger decided, thinking of the freckles all over her legs. They'd see them soon enough. Besides, she didn't feel like going into the closet to change clothes. Not yet, anyhow.

By the time she'd put her clothes away and shoved her suitcase under the bed, they heard a car pull up and car doors slam. Ginger quickly tossed her gum into the wastebasket so it wouldn't get on anyone's nerves.

"Are you girls decent?" Aunt Jennie asked in a cheerful voice as she knocked at the door.

"We are," Berkie said, hurrying to let her mother in.

Ginger remembered Aunt Jennie as soon as she saw her face over the grocery bags. She was even prettier than Berkie, with smooth golden blonde hair that curled under and blue-green eyes that looked at you like she really cared. Her nice smile was just like Grant's, too, which wasn't so surprising since he was her brother.

"Do you remember me from the wedding?" she asked.

"I do now," Ginger replied. "Except you weren't wearing blue jeans and a T-shirt."

"Or tennies!" Aunt Jennie said with a laugh. She plopped the grocery bags on her bed. "And you looked like a fairy-tale princess in your peach bridesmaid dress and halo of flowers. I think everyone in that church must have had tears in their eyes when you came down that aisle so . . . so bravely."

"You think so?" Ginger asked. No one had ever mentioned that it must have taken a lot of bravery.

23

"I know so. And I know Whom you depend upon for your courage, too. Now, how about a hug before the men get in here?"

Ginger hated hugging almost-strangers, but she gave in. Aunt Jennie, it turned out, was loving and cozy like Mom.

Grandfather had left the connecting door between the rooms ajar. The others must have just returned, too, because Ginger heard him welcoming Todd and Uncle Charlie in the "boys' room."

"Ladies," Grandfather said, knocking at the door, "I heard grocery bags rustling, and I've never been known to run at the sound of groceries. May we join the party?"

"Oh, Dad, come in!" Aunt Jennie said and gave her father a joyous hug. "I bought some dip and chips for a welcoming party. Charles, you remember Ginger, don't you?"

"How could I forget such a lovely redhead?" her uncle said, putting out a hand to shake.

"I remember you, too." Ginger smiled, but ignored his compliment as she shook his hand. "You're the one who looks like the father on 'Little House on the Prairie.'" He truly did, right down to the big grin and curly dark hair.

Uncle Charlie teased, "Actually, I don't look like him at all. They made that actor up to look like me, and then gave him my first name, too."

Everyone laughed, and Uncle Charlie turned to his son in the wheelchair. "We're welcomed to the girls'

24

side, Todd. This is your cousin Ginger . . . Ginger, this is Todd."

"Hi," Ginger said, feeling a little weird. Why was it that when she saw someone in a wheelchair, her eyes always pulled away?

"Hi," he replied, not looking very happy.

She tried to think of something to say.

Grandfather said, "We can contribute a few leftover ham sandwiches, fruit, carrot and celery sticks, and brownies, thanks to Ginger's Grandmother Trumbell."

"Wonderful!" Aunt Jennie said. "Todd, would you open these chips bags? And, Charles, would you bring us a chair to use as a serving table? I bought a few more soft drinks, too, to add to those in the cooler."

Todd flicked another look at Ginger, and she smiled at him.

He smiled, too, but his blue-green eyes stayed hard. Otherwise, he might have been handsome with his square, dimpled chin and curly brown hair. "If you don't mind, Mom," he said, "I'd really rather go lie down and read for a while."

"Sure, Todd," Aunt Jennie said uneasily.

"You don't have to look at me like that, Mom," Todd said. "Or the rest of you, either!" He whirled his wheelchair around and out of the room, slamming the connecting door behind him.

Ginger said, "I—I hope I didn't hurt his feelings."

Uncle Charlie drew a deep breath. "I'm sorry you have to see him like this," he said to her and Grandfather. "He's turned a little sullen lately. We hope the

25

'Go for It' climb might change his outlook." He carried a chair over to serve as a table between the beds. "If you'll excuse me, I'll see if he needs help."

Berkie ripped open the top of the chips bag, pressing her lips together hard, and Ginger hoped that her stepcousin wouldn't break down and cry.

When Uncle Charlie closed the door behind him, Grandfather said quietly, "Todd's well into his teens now. I expect that's where part of the trouble comes from. It's hard to accept limitations when we want so badly to be independent."

Aunt Jennie shook her head as she put out the dip. "Todd's part of why we started home schooling. He couldn't stand high school anymore. The kids ignored him, and he was so far ahead in most classes he said everything was boring-boring-boring. With my teaching background and Charlie's expertise in math and computers, things seemed to fall into place perfectly."

Grandfather asked, "Doesn't he want to continue home schooling, either?"

"No, he does like it best," Aunt Jennie replied. "He knows he can go back to a regular school anytime he likes."

"How about you, Berkeley?" Grandfather asked.

She nodded. "I guess I like home schooling best, too."

Grandfather asked Aunt Jennie, "And how about you?"

"I love it. And we feel it's what God wants us to do."

Ginger took a chip and scraped it through the onion

dip in a plastic cup, wishing she hadn't come. They'd probably invited Grandfather Gabriel in hopes that he could help with Todd's problems, she decided and bit into the chip.

They sat making small talk as they ate the chips, veggie sticks, and dip, and drank the soft drinks, but none of it tasted as good as usual.

Finally, Uncle Charlie returned to the room. "Hey, how about some music?" he asked and turned on the portable radio on top of the dresser. "One thing about radio in Yosemite, you're never worn out by dialing. There are only a few stations!"

A symphony to match the mountains filled the room, and Uncle Charlie went over to the windows and pulled the plaid draperies wide open. "Just look at those trees! Just look at that view!"

Nearby, a noisy jay squawked raucously.

Ginger felt as if things might get better. At least, Uncle Charlie was trying, and Aunt Jennie looked brighter. Berkie did, too. She remembered Grandfather once saying, "It only takes one member of a family to pull down the spirits of everyone else, *if* everyone else will allow it."

It didn't look as if Uncle Charlie would allow it, and she knew Grandfather sure wouldn't.

An hour later, at six o'clock, they decided to go to Yosemite Village for dinner. Uncle Charlie's maroon van was parked right next to the cabin in the handicapped space. When he opened the back of the van, there was a hydraulic lift that lowered to the ground. Todd rolled his wheelchair onto a platform and then was raised into the back of the van. To Ginger's surprise, half of the backseat was empty . . . a wheelchair space.

When Todd was in place, he shot Ginger a mean glance for watching, and she quickly turned away.

Since the van held only four people, Grandfather said, "I'll walk with the young ladies."

As they walked up the forested path toward the parking lot, Ginger asked Berkie, "How are you home schooling here?"

"We're working on Indian and nature study. I'm doing the ranger trip reports, and Todd's taking slides. Then we'll give a Yosemite program at a convalescent home in our neighborhood."

"Hey, that sounds neat! I thought you'd have to bring math workbooks and stuff like that along."

Berkie gave a little laugh. "Not in the summer! We don't have to do anything. There's plenty of workbook stuff to do at home the rest of the year! We try to do something special one day every month at the convalescent home, though."

Grandfather said, "Sounds like a fine idea. If I ever get old and have to go to a convalescent home, I hope you'll come entertain me with a program."

"You're not going to get old!" Ginger insisted, then kicked a beat-up pinecone across the dusty path.

"I appreciate your confidence!" he answered with a laugh.

As they passed his white Plymouth in the parking lot, he said, "Looks like we're acquiring half of Yosemite's dust."

Ginger grinned, knowing how he liked to keep his car clean. She stopped and wrote her initials, GAT, for Ginger Anne Trumbell in the dust on the back door, then BEA, for Berkeley Elizabeth Adamson.

Berkie darted a glance at Grandfather.

He chuckled and wrote MGG, for Matthew Grant Gabriel, his own initials, right next to theirs. "At long last, I own a monogrammed car!"

They laughed and walked on.

Grandfather was all right, Ginger thought, but she didn't like the idea of his getting really old.

When they were slightly ahead of him on the path, Ginger asked Berkie, "Are you doing home schooling because of Todd?"

Berkie nodded. "Don't tell anyone, though. It turns out that I really like it anyhow."

"I think I'd miss my friends at Santa Rosita Christian," Ginger decided.

"We go to a Christian school on Friday afternoons for youth activities, and there are group field trips, too. The best part is we don't have to get up at the crack of dawn to catch a school bus and spend forever riding one home. There's lots of extra time to do things we'd rather do."

"Like what?"

"Like I'm in Christian Community Theater. We just did Cinderella for thousands of kids in youth groups and Christian schools and scouting. And, last year, while everyone else was in school, we drove to Washington, D.C., on a family field trip for history. We help Mom put out a home-schooling newsletter to other families in the state, too."

"I didn't know there'd be such interesting things to do."

"If we really work hard, we can get our day's work done in four hours. There aren't other kids for Mom to teach. It's just one-on-one, so that saves a lot of time. We work extra so we can finish a week's work in four days, then we have a day off to do something special in our fields of interest."

"What are those?" Ginger asked, beginning to feel overwhelmed.

"Todd works Mondays at Dad's electronics plant. He does computer stuff like inventory control. And I'm volunteering at the hospital."

"You want to be a nurse or a doctor?"

Berkie nodded. "Pediatrics. You know, work with kids."

Probably because of Todd's injury, Ginger decided. She said, "I don't even know what I'll do when I finish school."

Berkie laughed. "Dad says if we pray for direction, God will tell us when the time comes."

"Yeah, I guess so."

"Want to go with Mom and me tomorrow on a ranger walk?"

"Sure," Ginger decided. "Hey, maybe I could write

a report on it, too, to use for school next fall!"

Ginger recognized Yosemite Village from when they'd driven in. It was all wooden buildings with lots of glass, and the open spaces were full of shrubs, native plants, and wildflowers in bloom. She remembered the Visitors Center and the post office, too, and the restaurants and shops.

"There's our van," Berkie said.

The maroon van was already parked in a handicapped space.

Berkie added, "They're going ahead and saving a table."

Inside the cafeteria, colorful banners hung from the high ceiling, and the huge windows on three sides looked out at the trees. They spotted Uncle Charlie, Aunt Jennie, and Todd just sitting down near one of the windows.

"You lead us through the line, Berkie," Grandfather said. "You know your way around here already."

Ginger got the same things Berkie chose: a salad, a slice of garlic bread, spaghetti and meatballs, and milk. They'd already decided to eat Gram's brownies for dessert later.

Ginger said to her cousin, "You have good taste!"

"Only because Mom's here," Berkie admitted with a grin.

When they arrived at the table, Ginger sat as far away from Todd as she could manage. She didn't feel very good about it, though, especially when it was time to say grace.

Grandfather prayed out loud, right in the middle of all of the other people in the cafeteria. "Heavenly Father," he began, "we praise You for the wonders of Your creation that we see here at Yosemite, and we thank You for allowing us to be here to see them. We thank You, too, for this bounty of food for our bodies' nourishment. And we ask, Heavenly Father, that You would allow us to reflect Your love to all of those around us. In Christ's name we pray. Amen."

Ginger was glad to see him take his blue plastic pillbox from his shirt pocket and take one of his pills. He was right on schedule today, one pill before every meal.

She glanced at Todd, and it looked like he was feeling a little better. She probably would feel unsure about mountain climbing, too, if she were stuck in a wheelchair.

She twirled strands of spaghetti around her fork thoughtfully. With the clatter of dishes and cafeteria trays all around them, she quietly asked Berkie, "Did Todd want to come here to go mountain climbing?"

"Sure," Berkie answered. "It was his idea in the first place." Cutting the spaghetti with her fork, she added, "He has to decide by Monday. Only five days!"

3

The next morning, Ginger was the first one from their cabin to go outside. Sunshine filtered through the trees and shimmered on the huge gray mountains, and the air smelled crisp with a slight scent of faraway campfires.

Standing on the deck, she drank a can of orange juice. At nearby cabins, a few people began to stir about, some heading down the log-lined paths toward the distant parking area. Only Uncle Charlie's maroon van was parked near a cabin because of the handicapped space.

After finishing the orange juice, she shoved a stick of gum into her mouth and watched two older boys step out of the next cabin, which was some distance away. They were dressed all in black and looked tough, like gang members. She chewed her gum hard and backed toward her cabin as they grooved along the path toward her.

"Man, ain't you crazy with that red hair?" the thin, tall one with dark wavy hair said to her.

The shorter one, probably his brother, said, "That ain't hair! That's a mop!"

Ginger clenched her fists. Much as she felt like backing away farther, she stood her ground.

"Don't you talk yet, little girl?" the older one asked.

Ginger snapped, "Why should I talk to you?"

She turned up her nose and started for the cabin. At least she hadn't given in entirely. She didn't even listen to what else they said. She guessed that it wouldn't be good.

When she looked back at them, they'd already forgotten about her and were heading on.

Moments later, she was glad to hear their own cabin door open. Turning, she watched Todd wheeling himself down the ramp, then rolling his wheelchair over the deck toward her.

"Hi," she said as he approached.

"I'm sorry I was so obnoxious yesterday," he said, not meeting her eyes.

"It's all right." She waited for him to give an excuse. When he didn't say anything, she added, "You were probably just tired. Grandfather and I sure were tired from driving all the way here yesterday. Did you see how he almost fell asleep when we were talking in the cabin after dinner?"

"Yeah," Todd said. He looked at the sunshine filtering through the trees. "Yeah, I guess I was tired."

Two cute girls about his age passed by on the path and, though he noticed them, they didn't even glance at him. It didn't matter that they ignored her, because she was younger, Ginger thought. But the way they ignored Todd, you'd have guessed he and the wheelchair were invisible.

You should have looked! she felt like yelling after them. *You'd have looked at him if he weren't in a wheelchair!*

With the sunlight gleaming on his dark wavy hair, he really was handsome. He wore jeans and a blue-green shirt the exact shade of his eyes. If he'd been sitting in a deck chair or on a bench, high school girls would notice how handsome he was.

Uncle Charlie stepped out of the cabin, holding the door open for the others. "Everyone ready for breakfast?" he asked, darting a strange look at her and Todd.

So that was it! Ginger guessed. *Uncle Charlie had sent Todd out ahead to apologize to her! Probably he'd apologized to Grandfather inside.* She was sure of it and gave her gum a loud crack. So much for her feeling sorry for Todd!

Her uncle asked, "Want to wheel or ride in the van to the cafeteria this morning, Todd?"

"Ride," Todd said, darting a fast glance at Ginger. He wondered if she thought he was lazy, she realized. At least what she thought of him must matter.

"Fine," his father was saying. "We'll beat the others there and save a table." He turned to Grandfather Gabriel. "Are you sure you don't want to ride?"

"Thanks, but I need my morning walk," Grandfather answered. "If we weren't at such a high altitude, I'd be jogging and beat you there!"

Uncle Charlie laughed. He opened the back of the van and pushed a button that let down the hydraulic lift for Todd and the wheelchair.

"And how are you this fine morning, Ginger?" Grandfather asked with a pat on her shoulder.

"Ready to explore Yosemite!" she replied.

Berkie and Aunt Jennie grinned, and they all fell into step as they headed down the dusty path toward the village. All of them wore jeans, even Grandfather, and they had on sweatshirts since the air was still cool.

Aunt Jennie turned to Ginger. "We thought we might go on a ranger walk in the forest this morning while the men are out snapping pictures. Then this afternoon, you and Berkie can go bicycling to Happy Isles or horseback riding or rafting. How does that sound?"

"All right!" Ginger said.

Berkie asked, "Can we go to a campfire program tonight?"

"If we're not exhausted," her mother said. "We all had a good rest last night."

Grandfather said, "Sorry I was such a spoilsport, but the drive up here was tiring."

"I needed the rest myself," Aunt Jennie replied.

"Just look at this view!" Grandfather said with a sweeping gesture toward the meadows and mountains. "The naturalist John Muir rhapsodized about the mountains with 'their brows in the sky, a thousand flowers leaning confidingly at their feet.' "

"The flowers look more 'rising up' than leaning,' " Ginger decided. "But I like the mountains' 'brows in the sky.' "

Uncle Charlie honked as they drove by, and everyone waved at them. Ginger noticed that Todd sat alone in the back in his wheelchair. He sat there stiffly, without waving, and she wondered if he even noticed the mountains or the meadows all bright with wildflowers.

When the van moved on, she called out to the others, "Hey, look, three . . . no, it's five deer!" The deer were grazing in the meadow as if there weren't even hikers, bicyclers, and cars all around.

Berkie said, "They're out every morning."

"All right!" Ginger said. "It's sure beautiful here!"

When they arrived in the village, the wooden buildings were shaded from the morning sunshine under the trees. It was beautiful, but in a different way this morning.

Inside the cafeteria, park visitors bustled with renewed energy; trays and dishes clattered, and people chattered excitedly in different languages. Ginger felt a surge of excitement about the day ahead.

"There they are," Berkie said, waving at her father and Todd, who were already settled by the window.

Aunt Jennie said, "I'm starved. Let's get in line before it gets longer. You first, Ginger."

Ginger grabbed a tray, and, as they moved through the cafeteria line, she decided on blueberry pancakes and milk.

After passing the cashier, Ginger headed through the crowded room to the table. Like last night, Todd sat at the head of it to make room for his wheelchair, and Uncle Charlie sat to one side. It seemed she had no choice but to sit beside Todd. "Okay if I sit here?" she asked him.

"You don't have to if you don't want to," he replied and kept on eating.

"I know that!" she half-snapped, then was sorry her temper had gotten the best of her.

No one else seemed to notice since Uncle Charlie had gotten up to help Aunt Jennie with her tray.

Ginger sat down in a huff, in no mood to hear grace.

Sitting at the other end of the table, Grandfather bowed his head and began to pray.

Ginger ducked her head and, as he prayed, she peeked at Todd. His head was bowed but she wondered if he were praying.

She tuned back in to the prayer and, when Grandfather finished, added a silent, *Lord, help me to be kind to Todd today! Please help me!*

Everyone was already talking when she looked up and Todd said in an undertone, "Well, aren't you Miss Pious?"

Ginger blinked at him as if she didn't understand,

but she knew exactly what he meant. He thought she was pretending—and she sure wasn't. Besides, Grandfather said pretending to be a Christian didn't do any good.

She asked as nicely as she could, "Are you a Christian?"

He shot back, "None of your business!"

Ginger glanced up and found Uncle Charlie looking at them, and she quickly began to eat her pancakes. Just see if she'd ever sit by Todd again! And because of him, she'd forgotten to watch Grandfather to see if he'd taken his pill.

An hour later, Ginger felt better. For one thing, the men had taken off in the van to get pictures of wildflowers blooming in the meadows, and she was watching the "One Day in Yosemite" video program in the Visitors Center with Berkie and Aunt Jennie. Just realizing how many forests, waterfalls, meadows, and mountains there were to see and the exciting activities to do lifted her spirits joyously.

Aunt Jennie had registered them for a ranger walk, so after buying postcards at the Visitors Center, they headed for the outdoor Indian museum, where Berkie had come yesterday for her Indian report.

Ginger didn't know what to expect, but it was just like an early Yosemite Indian village must have been. There were tepee-shaped bark houses and, high on posts, pine-covered shelters for storing acorns. Indians sat demonstrating basket weaving, beadwork, and arrow making. "It's like walking into an old Indian village," she said to Aunt Jennie.

The Indian woman in front of them weaving a basket smiled as if to say, *That's the way it's supposed to be.*

Ginger smiled back at her.

They moved on through the village, and, after a while, she pressed a push-button recording that told about the Indians. "They called themselves Awaneechees—'the people of the deep, grassy valley'—and they lived in Yosemite Valley during the summers. When winter storms came, they moved to the lower, warmer foothills. They caught fish in the streams and had deer, bear, and squirrel for meat and fur. They ate acorns, seeds, berries, bulbs, and roots. . . ."

As they wandered through the Indian village, Berkie said, "I wonder if they hate us for changing everything on them."

"I can't say I'd blame them too much," Aunt Jennie replied. "Unfortunately, the history of human beings is full of change. Even our lives change, no matter how hard we try to stop events."

Like Todd's accident changing his life, Ginger thought.

As they moved on, she heard a boy jeer, "There's that crazy redhead!"

She turned and, sure enough, it was the two boys from the next cabin. She was glad Aunt Jennie gave them a curious look, because they moved on without saying another word.

"Do you know them?" Berkie asked.

Ginger shook her head. "I saw them this morning. They're in the cabin next to ours."

"Are they really?" Berkie asked.

" 'Fraid so."

Just before ten o'clock, Aunt Jennie drove Grandfather's car to the lower Yosemite Falls parking lot. They parked just in time, too, because their group was already surrounding the ranger. He was dressed in a gray shirt, khaki pants and khaki tie, and wore a tan Stetson hat. "Good morning," he said and introduced himself. "Where are you ladies from?"

Aunt Jennie said, "We're from the San Francisco area, and my niece, Ginger, is from Santa Rosita."

Ginger smiled, glad she hadn't been called a stepniece, which didn't sound quite as friendly.

"Welcome to our forest walk," he said. "I think we're ready to set out now."

Nearby, Yosemite Falls roared over the rocks. The air had grown warmer, and the sun felt good on Ginger's face.

"This is Ponderosa pine," the ranger said. He held up a bundle of three-pronged long needles, then began to tell them how to know the difference between pine, fir, cedar, and oak trees. "And this white flowering tree is dogwood—"

Berkie was taking notes in a spiral notebook for her report, but Ginger decided she wouldn't write a report after all. She just stood in the midst of God's creation and enjoyed it.

41

"The Yosemite Valley used to be a lake," the ranger was saying, "so you're really standing on a lake floor. Yosemite was discovered in 1851—"

Ginger only half-heard him, listening instead to the stillness of the forest. Here the treetops shaded them from the sun, but in places golden rays broke through. She wanted always to remember how beautiful the forest was.

"Is fire a friend or a foe of the forest?" the ranger asked, and people in their group guessed at the answer.

"Foe," Ginger decided, but she was wrong.

"Lightning fires are good for the forest and usually go out by themselves, only burning little patches," the ranger said. "Human fires, however, begin in the canyons, and air currents sweep them up into great fires. That's why we have to put them out as quickly as possible. Nature's ways and man's ways are so often very different."

Aunt Jennie murmured to Ginger and Berkie, "He means *God's* ways and man's ways are so often very different."

Aunt Jennie was thinking about God, too, here in the forest, Ginger thought.

Someone in the group asked the ranger a question, and Ginger only heard his answer. "Yes, it's a shame, but we do have more serious park visitor problems in the national parks nowadays, too," he said. "Unfortunately, people bring their troubles with them."

Those boys in the next cabin were just the trouble type! Ginger thought.

As the group followed the ranger along the forest path, a strange squirrel ran up and down a tree, then somersaulted and back flipped in the air.

"Look at that!" people called out.

"A chickaree," the ranger told them. "They're full of energy and busier than squirrels."

Everyone laughed as they watched the squirrellike animal somersault and flip in the air again.

Ginger laughed herself and said to Berkie, "God surely did make a lot of different animals."

"He surely did," Berkie agreed.

Their eyes met, and they smiled at each other.

"Are you all Christians?" Ginger asked.

Berkie beamed, then turned a little too serious. "We are except . . . I don't know about Todd. Lately, he seems to have given up on God. We thought the mountain climbing might help."

"I wish he were here with us now to see the forest," Ginger said.

She'd feel a lot better about him if she knew he still believed. Faith had changed everything for her when things seemed hopeless. But it couldn't be a wishy-washy faith. You really had to grab hold of God.

4

Ginger and Berkie sat in the backseat as Aunt Jennie drove them through the valley and over the Merced River to Camp Curry. A wooden sign said, "Curry Village, founded in 1899." Arrows on the rustic sign pointed to the gift shop, Mountain Shop, hamburger stand, bike rentals, mountaineering school, and dining pavilion.

"Look, tent cabins!" Ginger said.

"We stayed in them a long time ago," Berkie answered. "Before Todd's accident. There are wooden cabins, too."

"Do you come to Yosemite a lot?" Ginger asked.

"We used to," Berkie said.

"I guess a lot of things changed after Todd's accident, didn't they?"

Berkie nodded. "They sure did."

Aunt Jennie finally found a parking space close to Uncle Charlie's maroon van in the handicapped-only space. They parked and hurried out toward a brown barnlike building with colorful umbrellas on the deck.

Ginger remarked, "It looks like an outdoor restaurant at a nice shopping center, except it's surrounded by the forest and mountains." She glanced ahead. "What's that stage with wooden benches in front of it for?"

"Ranger talks in the evening," Berkie answered.

Aunt Jennie said, "Maybe we'll come here one night."

Uncle Charlie, Grandfather, and Todd waved at them from the Meadow Deck by the hamburger stand. It was a busy place, selling sandwiches, french fries, ice cream, and drinks.

The men took their orders and stood in line, while Ginger, Berkie, Todd, and Aunt Jennie waited for a table.

"I'm starved!" Ginger said as she eyed people finishing their hamburgers and drinks.

"Me, too," Berkie agreed.

Todd shot a disgusted look at them from his wheelchair, but it was the kind any older brother, handicapped or not, might give younger girls, Ginger decided.

Aunt Jennie said, "I've got plenty of fruit in the cooler, so we can skip dessert."

They got a table just as Grandfather and Uncle Charlie arrived with the cardboard carriers of burgers, french fries, and drinks. As they settled at the table, Ginger made sure she sat between Berkie and Aunt Jennie—not by Todd.

Uncle Charlie said, "We thought it'd be a good idea to meet here, so you girls are next to the bike rental place. It's not too far from Happy Isles."

Ginger unwrapped her cheeseburger. "How will we get back to the cabin? It seems far away to me."

"Not so far that you couldn't walk," Grandfather assured her. "And you can always catch the tram around the park. We'll drive to Happy Isles later so Todd can get more pictures, and we'll see if you're there for a ride back then."

Ginger felt Todd looking at her, and she busied herself with her french fries and ketchup.

Berkie told her, "Mom and I hiked to Happy Isles the afternoon we came, so I remember the way around. I've already written about it in my report."

"What is Happy Isles anyway?" Ginger asked.

"Where the Merced River comes over Vernal and Nevada Falls, and flows into the valley," Berkie explained. "They have junior and senior ranger programs there for school kids. Whole bus loads come sometimes. There's a nature center and all kinds of things. You'll like it!"

Ginger hoped so. She took a big bite of her cheeseburger. It was delicious, loaded with mustard, ketchup, and pickle slices. Seeing Happy Isles and the waterfalls sounded exciting all right. Besides, she and Berkie could be on their own.

Three men walked past the deck, carrying rope and other climbing gear. Probably climbers on the way to the mountaineering school. "Tomorrow we'll be on El Capitán!" one said.

Ginger glanced at Todd.

"What are you looking at me for?" he asked.

She shook her head. "Nothing." She knew, though, that he was only acting as if he hadn't heard the climbers. He had until Monday to decide if he were climbing on the "Go for It" expedition in his wheelchair. It was only four days away.

When they'd finished lunch, she and Berkie walked to the bike rental shop. Before long they were on their rented bicycles and yelling "Goodbye! Goodbye, all!" to the others.

Grandfather called after them, "Got a map?"

"I've got one!" Berkie answered. She wore a denim bow in her hair to match her jeans, and the bow looked so jaunty as they rode along through the forest's sunshine and shadows that Ginger thought she'd buy one, too, when she had a chance.

After a while, Berkie yelled back, "You okay?"

"Yeah! It's wonderful here!" Wildflowers bloomed in the tall grasses along the bicycle trail, and the forest and mountains were bright with sunshine. "I was thinking maybe next year my family could meet your family here!"

"That'd really be fun," Berkie replied.

They rode past forests, campgrounds, and colorful meadows. Before long, the road changed. A sign said,

"Only handicapped-person vehicles allowed," and, since there were none, Ginger caught up with Berkie and they rode side by side.

"Hey, listen!" Ginger said, hearing a subdued roar.

"It's the Merced River. And there's the Happy Isles Nature Center. I took notes there for my report."

"There are bus loads of school kids, all right," Ginger said. Groups of kids sat with rangers and teachers listening to nature talks, some of them not listening too hard. Others followed rangers on walks on forest trails.

"Let's go up the trail to Vernal and Nevada Falls first," Berkie suggested. "That's my favorite place. There's a bike rack near the trail."

The Merced River rushed around small wooded islands and the waters met again in a merry flow just before the bridge. "I see why it's called Happy Isles," Ginger said.

"It makes me feel happy just to be here," Berkie agreed.

They rode over the bridge and parked their bikes in the bike rack. A sign pointed them onward: "Vernal and Nevada Falls Nature Trail." After a while, they stopped at the edge of the river to watch again.

Frothy water crashed over huge boulders, filling the whole valley with the sound of rushing water. Ginger said, "It sounds like the streams are shouting for joy and splashing up their water like hands clapping."

Berkie rolled her blue eyes skyward, and Ginger laughed. "That's what comes from being around Grandfather Gabriel. He's always describing things so they sound straight from the Bible."

"Now don't you laugh at me," Berkie said, "but I think the water sounds like it's telling the boulders, 'Wake up! Wake up! Can't you see this is exciting? here?!' "

"It sounds like that, too, all right."

A moment later, Ginger stopped in her tracks. "Look over there! It's those boys from the next cabin!"

"They look a little scary in those black outfits," Berkie said. "What on earth are they doing?"

Ginger watched as the boys pulled clothes from a trash container as if they were magicians. It turned out to be their black jackets and other stuff they'd stashed there. "Let's get out of here!" she said, and they hurried on.

After a while, she glanced back. "They're headed down the path. I don't think they saw us."

"Thank goodness!" Berkie said. "Come on, wait till you see the falls."

As they made their way up the trail, the valley filled with the roar of falling water. The trail became steeper as the roar grew louder, until at last they rounded a curve and a sheet of water thundered down over the cliffs, making the ground beneath their feet shake.

At long last they rounded a bend and saw a twisting curtain of water whose thundering tones boomed through the valley. Vernal Falls slid over a great, dark cliff, then crashed into giant rocks below, spraying rainbows in the mist and foam. Drenched by the mist, Ginger felt she was in a kaleidoscope of changing rainbows. "It's wonderful!" she yelled, her voice lost in the roar.

She and Berkie stood with their arms out, then started whirling in the mist.

"Let's stay here forever!" Ginger yelled, still whirling.

Berkie stuck her fingers in her ears. "It helps!"

Ginger closed her ears, too, and they both stood looking again at the rainbows in the mist, getting drenched.

"I'm going to remember this forever!" Ginger yelled.

Berkie nodded, her hair plastered down to her scalp.

After a while, Berkie asked, "You want to climb higher? Nevada Falls is even better, except you get drenched going up!"

"Let's go!" Ginger decided.

They laughed and headed higher up the Mist Trail, getting wetter yet.

The trail grew steeper and steeper, and the girls passed older people resting on downed logs along the edges. Ginger kept up with Berkie, climbing until both of them were huffing and puffing too hard even for laughing.

As they rounded a corner, Berkie announced, "Nevada Falls!"

A mighty sheet of water roared over a cliff, changing from green to purplish gray and white, then dashed onto giant boulders into clouds of spray and beat its way downriver.

"Wow!" Ginger yelled over the roar. "It doesn't have rainbows, but it's sure . . . magnificent!"

They stood looking at the waterfall for a long time, then Berkie shouted, "We'd better start down!"

"Yeah. But I want to come again!" Ginger returned.

"We will!"

It was a long way downhill to Vernal Falls's thundering roar, where they stopped for another look at the waterfall and the rainbows in its mist.

When they arrived down at the bottom of the trail, Berkie said, "Hey, look who's here!"

Ginger looked up and saw Grandfather Gabriel, Aunt Jennie, Uncle Charlie, and Todd enjoying the Happy Isle scene.

As they hurried over, Aunt Jennie saw them. "Well, if it isn't two drenched rats!" she laughed. "What did you do, ride down the waterfalls?"

Ginger could imagine how she must look with her red hair soaking wet. She joked, "We rode over them in a barrel."

"You must have left your heads out!" Uncle Charlie said.

Everyone laughed except Todd, who was snapping pictures from his wheelchair.

Ginger said to him, "Would you like me to push your wheelchair up the trail a ways so you can get pictures? It's wonderful up there."

She thought he was going to refuse, then he seemed to change his mind. "Okay," he said, his blue-green eyes meeting hers. "But I can wheel myself where it's not too steep."

"Sure," she answered. "You tell me what to do."

Berkie and the others looked surprised, then followed along behind them.

After a while, the trail began to rise, and, strong as Todd's arms and shoulders were, he was wearing out. "Okay . . . you can push now for a while."

Ginger pushed the wheelchair slowly up the steep path. Even if they didn't get very far, it'd be worth it for Todd to see as much as he could and to take pictures.

"You can stop here now," Todd said. "I want to get those trees in the picture."

Ginger stopped, and he snapped a picture.

She turned to see where the others were, but they were looking at something along the trail.

"Okay, thanks," he said. He glanced back. "What are they looking at?"

"Probably a chickaree stripping a pine cone. The ranger told us about them this morning. You want to go higher?"

"If you're not getting tired," he answered.

"Who me, tired?" It was the friendliest he had been so far, and she wasn't about to stop now. "Okay, hold on!"

The trail bumped along, but it wasn't too bad. Pushing the wheelchair along reminded her of the "Go for It" video she'd seen about pushing one of the wheelchair kids up the mountain. Maybe someday she'd help push people in wheelchairs on a real mountain climbing adventure.

"Way to go!" said some hikers coming down.

The trail grew steeper and steeper with rocks and

roots sticking out here and there. An elderly couple with walking sticks hiked down carefully, and Ginger stopped, pushing a little toward the edge to let them pass.

Todd snapped another picture. "Okay."

"Let's go!" Ginger said.

She pushed the wheelchair onward, not seeing the rock at the edge of the path. Suddenly a wheel bumped over it.

"Yii!" she cried out, struggling with the wheelchair.

Todd yelled, "Hold it!"

She held on with all of her might. "I can't!"

Todd and the wheelchair tipped sideways over the edge, sliding down the forested hillside while she ran after it. "Help!!! Someone, help!!!" she shouted.

She half-ran, half-skidded through the ferns and underbrush toward the wheelchair, which had stopped against a huge tree. She grabbed hold of the tree to keep from falling farther herself. "Todd, are you all right?"

His forehead and arms were scraped and bleeding, but he opened his eyes and nodded with resignation. "I'm not dead yet, if that's what you mean. I've probably got a broken leg or two and don't even know it."

"I'm really sorry!" she almost bawled.

"Yeah . . . I guess you must be! See if you can get back up the hill and get my dad to help."

"And leave you here?"

"Believe me, I'm not going anywhere!" he said unhappily.

"Okay." She started up the hill, holding onto

branches and tree trunks, hot tears under her eyelids. She couldn't cry now! she warned herself. Not now . . . not now!

She was just nearing the trail's edge when Uncle Charlie came running. "You all right?" he asked Ginger, pulling her up as he took in the scene below. "Somebody said a wheelchair went over—"

"It tipped on a rock . . . it just tipped!"

"Is Todd all right?"

"He says so. He sent me for help."

Uncle Charlie started down the hillside toward Todd. "Tell Berkie to get the rope from the van. She'd better ask for a rescue team, too. We're going to need more help."

Berkie and Aunt Jennie came running, Grandfather Gabriel just behind them, and Ginger had to explain again. She'd never in her life felt so awful. Worst of all, she had a feeling Todd would never do the "Go for It" climb now!

5

In bed the next morning, Ginger wanted to die as she remembered yesterday's disaster: first, the wheelchair tipping out of control, then slipping down the ferny hillside. As if that weren't bad enough, the rescue team had carried Todd up on a stretcher while a crowd gathered around them to stare.

"Except for a few scrapes, he seems fine," the man in charge had said. "It was a nice, soft bed of ferns to slide on. But we need to take him to the clinic to be absolutely certain he's in as good shape as we think."

Uncle Charlie and Aunt Jennie had followed the ambulance in Grandfather's car, and Grandfather had driven the van so Ginger and Berkie could return their rented bicycles. Then they'd driven to the clinic, too.

Ginger burrowed deeper under the covers, wishing it had all been a nightmare. When she opened her eyes again, though, she was still in the cabin and knew the disaster was real. The only good thing was that Todd hadn't been hurt, and he'd been back in the cabin in time for dinner.

Everyone had tried to jolly him up with "You're a tough bird," and "You're tougher than you think," but it hadn't helped Ginger much. Worst of all, he'd given her such a hateful look that it had hurt her heart even more.

"Are you awake, Ginger?" Aunt Jennie asked from her bed across the room.

"Yeah," Ginger replied, seeing Berkie pull the covers up over her head. "But I wish I were dead."

"It really wasn't your fault any more than it was ours," her aunt said. "We shouldn't have let you get ahead of us, but we thought it might be a good thing for Todd to be with you."

Ginger rose up on her elbows. "To be with me?"

"Yes, to see how spunky and adventurous you are."

Ginger swallowed hard. "I sure don't feel very spunky or adventurous now."

The truth was she felt like going home instead of facing Todd again. Last night hadn't been so bad, because Grandfather had taken her and Berkie out for pizza, and Uncle Charlie had bought take-out food from the market for the rest of them. By the time they'd returned, Todd was reading in bed, and she hadn't even offered to say good-night to him.

Aunt Jennie said, "Not even the camera or the wheelchair were damaged, so I don't want you feeling guilty over a little accident."

Little accident! Ginger thought. *There'd been nothing little about it!* Worse, she recalled the "Go for It" video when one of the wheelchair climbers had fallen. He'd been a grown-up, though, and had gone right on up the mountain again.

Aunt Jennie got out of bed and pulled the plaid draperies aside for a moment. "It's beautiful again. Wonder what we could do for excitement today?"

"Stay in bed," Ginger suggested morosely. "I want to spend the whole day in bed."

Berkie sat up in the middle bed. "Come on, Ginger. It's not the first time Todd's tipped over in the wheelchair."

"You're kidding—"

Berkie shook her head. "He fell over a couple of times at school and when he's played wheelchair basketball. Usually we don't have to get a rescue team, though. I thought the men were handsome, didn't you?"

"Why, Berkie!" her mother said with a surprised laugh.

Ginger sat up herself. "I didn't even notice!"

Berkie's lips curved up in a Cheshire cat grin. "I knew that would get your attention."

And change the subject, Ginger thought gratefully.

Outside the cabin, she kept her distance from Todd again. Everything went fine until an elderly lady passed by. "Aren't you the young man who fell down the hill in your wheelchair?" she asked Todd, eyeing the scrapes on his forehead.

Todd looked at her like he couldn't believe a stranger would walk up and mention it.

Uncle Charlie said, "He's fine now. We appreciate your concern."

"He's a brave young man," she said. She moved on, pleased, as if she'd done her good deed for the day.

There were other people around in wheelchairs, but none that Ginger had seen with scrapes on their foreheads like Todd. As for his arms, they were covered with a long-sleeved sweatshirt, and she didn't even want to guess how bad they might be.

Grandfather said, "We've decided to split up for the day. Todd and I will stay down in the valley, and Uncle Charlie will drive you ladies up to Glacier Point."

Ginger guessed they were doing it that way to separate her from Todd—and maybe to give everyone more space.

Grandfather said, "Ginger, don't forget, tonight's our date at the Ahwahnee Hotel. I've made dinner reservations for seven o'clock."

"Okay," she answered. Probably he was taking her tonight so she'd feel better.

On the way out to the car, Aunt Jennie slipped her arm around Ginger's shoulders and drew her aside. "I hope you're not feeling as unhappy inside as you look on the outside today," she said. "I was serious when I said I don't want you feeling guilty about yesterday."

58

Ginger swallowed hard.

"Just think how guilty I'd always feel if I let myself," her aunt continued. "I'm the one who was driving the car during the real accident. I could ruin my life and the whole family's if I were forever saying, 'You should have seen the other car coming at us sooner,' or dozens of other things."

Ginger nodded unhappily.

"Let's see you smile, Ginger Anne Trumbell," her aunt said, her blue eyes hopeful.

It took awhile, but finally Ginger managed to turn her lips up a little.

"That's better," her aunt said, giving Ginger's shoulders a squeeze. "In fact, it's the best smile I've seen on your face today. The sooner we can put yesterday's mishap behind us, the happier we'll all be. What do you think?"

Ginger nodded again, this time more hopefully. Mom always said to put bad things behind you as soon as possible, and Grandfather always said, "Learn from the past, then go on into the future. If God's always willing to forgive us and give us a fresh start, we have to forgive ourselves, too."

Her aunt was looking at her, and Ginger said, "Okay."

She did feel better and, when they set off in the car, Uncle Charlie announced, "It's going to be a great day."

Ginger hoped so.

At first, she stared quietly out the window at the passing scenery, and Berkie asked polite questions about Ginger's family. Ginger felt better just talking about Mom, Grant, Joshua, Lilabet, and baby Mattie, then telling about her friends at Santa Rosita Christian, especially her best friend, Katie.

They drove higher and higher on the curving road, following the Glacier Point signs. Finally they arrived at Glacier Point and climbed out of the car to view Yosemite from the top.

From high among the majestic mountain peaks, the valley below appeared amazingly small; the Merced River looked like a winding thread through the meadows, and cars were no more than moving specks. Even Yosemite Falls, which was so impressive down in the valley, seemed a miniature waterfall.

Uncle Charlie said to Ginger, "It puts a different perspective on things, doesn't it?"

"It sure does," Ginger agreed, knowing he meant more than just the way Yosemite looked from high in the mountains. He meant what Grandfather Gabriel called taking a long view of things. Yesterday's disaster with Todd and the wheelchair was already beginning to fade.

Berkie was writing in her blue notebook for her report.

"How will you describe Glacier Point?" Ginger asked.

Berkie shook her head. "It's not easy. What do you think about a panorama of great mountaintops?"

"How about a panorama of magnificent mountaintops?" Ginger suggested.

"Hey, that does sound better," Berkie said and scribbled it down.

That afternoon when they arrived back at the cabin, Ginger felt better, especially since Todd and Grandfather Gabriel weren't there. She glanced at the next cabin and was glad to see that their neighboring nasties weren't around either.

As they unlocked the cabin door, Berkie said, "Let's go swimming."

"Okay," Ginger said. "In the pool, I hope."

"Not in the river!" Berkie agreed. "That water is freezing." She turned to her mother. "Mom, may we?"

"Of course. It would be nice for your father and me to have the afternoon to ourselves."

Uncle Charlie grinned at her. "Are you up to hiking?"

Aunt Jennie laughed. "Not more than five or six miles. See you later, girls! Don't go into the pool unless there's a lifeguard on duty."

"Oh, Mom!" Berkie replied.

As soon as Aunt Jennie and Uncle Charlie left, Ginger grabbed her green one-piece suit from her suitcase and started to undress, tennies first.

"I'll use the dressing room," Berkie said, embarrassed.

"You're modest," Ginger guessed.

"Yeah, I suppose I am."

"I am a little, too," Ginger confessed.

With Berkie dressing in the big closet, Ginger was in her suit and had her tennies back on in no time. Probably Berkie was doing the balancing act it took to dress in the small closet dressing room.

Ginger grabbed her towel from the bathroom, then sat down on the edge of her bed. Waiting, she noticed a yellow brochure on top of the chest of drawers and picked it up. "The MountainEAR" it said. "Summit Adventure."

She thumbed through it, looking at a picture of a disabled boy Todd's age climbing a mountain, then at a half-page of letters titled "What Others Are Saying."

The first one said, "Thank you for opening the door for Sandy to be part of the 'Go for It' trip. It was the beginning of a major turnaround in his life. He really and truly gave his life to the Lord there, and he's on the life-changing journey. It's what we've been praying for."

Another said, "I wouldn't trade the time I spent with Summit for the world! I learned more about myself, about my strengths and weaknesses than I thought I could ever learn in five days! I know now that I can face my fears and overcome any obstacle through Christ."

Another person wrote, "Now I understand that we must depend on each other for encouragement. That we believers are all sisters and brothers, thanks to Jesus!"

Berkie came out of the dressing room in a blue one-piece suit. "What are you reading?"

Ginger lifted the newsletter. "About the 'Go for It!' trip. Todd *has* to go on it . . . he *has* to!"

"I know it," Berkie answered. "The trouble is, he doesn't like others to help him, especially strangers. I've been praying and praying about it."

"I haven't, but now I see how important it is. Let's pray about it together right now."

As Ginger reached for her cousin's hands, Berkie gave her a peculiar look.

"I guess you're not used to praying like this—like we do at Santa Rosita Christian," Ginger said.

Berkie shook her head. "It's all right with me, though."

"Okay," Ginger said and bowed her head. "Heavenly Father," she began, then took a deep, calming breath. "You know how terrible I still feel about letting Todd's wheelchair tip yesterday . . . and I remember now that I haven't given thanks to You in spite of it! I do thank You now in that and in everything else in my life."

She paused, trying to think how to pray for Todd. "You know how Todd doesn't want others, especially strangers, to help him much. We pray that You'll change that in him . . . and give him the courage to go on 'Go for It!' We pray in Jesus' name and thank You, Father. Amen."

She let loose of Berkie's hands, and they looked at each other hopefully.

"Amen," Berkie said and nodded.

Later, as they set out down the forested path, Berkie said, "I guess with Grandfather living near you, and Uncle Grant being principal of the Christian high school, you learn a lot about God and about praying."

"Yeah, I've learned a lot, and I haven't even been a

Christian one year. The most surprising thing I've learned is that being a Christian is a real adventure. You wouldn't believe some of the things that have happened to me already."

"Like what?" Berkie asked.

"Like playing guardian angel for the most awful girl," Ginger answered, "and having a miracle happen."

"We need a miracle for Todd!" Berkie said.

"Grandfather always says that God still does miracles, mainly for people who really hold on tight to Him. Do you have a Bible study in your home school?"

Berkie nodded. "Both Mom and Dad always begin the day's lessons with a psalm."

"We try to at breakfast, too. We just did Psalm 37. You know, 'The Lord delights in the way of the man whose steps he has made firm; though he stumble, he will not fall, for the Lord upholds him with his hand.' "

"I wish Todd would learn that one," Berkie said.

"You know what I just thought? He could really have been hurt if he'd slid farther down that hillside. Maybe it was God who stopped him with that tree."

Berkie shrugged. "Maybe."

Ginger looked out at the wildflowers, the forest, and the mountains all around them. "Maybe his just seeing how beautiful God made things here at Yosemite will help."

"I hope so," Berkie said. "Todd used to be lots different. Even though he was in a wheelchair, the teachers at our middle school said he was a born leader. Then he went to high school and everything changed, maybe because it was so big and there were so many kids. The boys were so physical, too. You know, wrestling around and giving high fives. And most of them were interested in girls, too. Todd felt sort of left out."

"I think his climbing a mountain would help," Ginger said.

"I do, too."

At the swimming pool, there were lots of kids crowding the bright blue water and the pool deck. Some were little and with their parents, but most were middle or high school age, and none payed much attention to the girls.

Ginger threw her towel in the corner. "Come on, let's dive in! It's not so crowded at the deep end."

"All right." Berkie tossed her towel on top of Ginger's, and they headed for the deep end. "Are you a good swimmer?"

"Not so good yet," Ginger answered. "I just learned last summer, but I've been swimming every day since school's been out. Grant says it's balm for our nerves with a new baby in the house. Are you good?"

"Just okay," Berkie said, then dove off perfectly from the pool's edge.

Ginger decided to hold her nose and jump in.

The water was cool, but she felt warmer as she swam around in the uncrowded deep end. After a while, she grabbed hold of the pool's edge for a rest.

Berkie came to join her, and they pushed their wet hair back off their faces.

A little kid was bawling by the pool's shallow end,

and they glanced over to see what was wrong with him. Two big boys were thrashing and splashing around so much that some of the other little kids were escaping up the pool steps, too.

The lifeguard lifted his megaphone and called out, "Let's not have so much rough stuff in the pool."

The two troublemakers pretended they hadn't heard him. They turned away unconcerned, looking at the deep end. "Hey," one of them yelled, "it's that crazy redhead!"

Ginger cringed as everyone stared at her.

"Yeah, that's her," the other boy agreed.

Berkie asked under her breath, "Are they who I think?"

Ginger nodded. "The boys from the next cabin."

"Oh, no—" Berkie said.

The two boys got out of the pool by the steps, and Ginger wasn't surprised to see that they even wore black swim trunks. They slicked back their dark hair and started around the deck toward them.

"I don't like the looks of them," Berkie remarked.

"I don't either," Ginger admitted.

"Hey, look at them freckles on you, Redhead," the older, taller boy said as they approached.

The younger one gave a laugh. "Bet you got freckles clear down to your toes!"

Ginger shot them her most huffy look. "Come on," she said to Berkie, and they swam off across the pool.

They'd no more than arrived, though, and the boys were there. "Come on, Redhead," they said, "tell us the name of your pretty friend."

Ginger didn't even bother to look at them and swam across the pool again.

This time when she grabbed hold of the edge, the older boy stepped on her hand with his bare foot.

"Hey!" she yelled and pulled her hand loose.

The lifeguard called out, "Behave over there, or I'll have to eject you boys from the pool!"

"We'll be good, lifeguard!" the younger one said in a phony voice. "We promise we'll be good!"

They sat down on the pool deck next to Ginger and Berkie. "I'm Kyle," the older one said, "and this is my brother, Curt. What's your—"

Berkie tugged on Ginger's arm. "Come on, let's swim."

"Good idea!" Ginger said and took off with Berkie across the pool.

When they arrived out of breath at the other end, the boys were already there, too.

"What's wrong with you two?" Ginger asked angrily. "Don't you know how to swim?"

The boys darted fast glances at each other, and she knew she'd hit on the truth. "So that's why you're bugging everyone!" she shot at them, then turned and swam away again.

When she grabbed the far edge again, she saw the boys leaving the pool area.

"Good riddance," Berkie said as she swam up beside her.

"Yeah," Ginger agreed, except at that very moment,

both boys turned to shoot a hateful look at them.

Ginger had a sinking feeling that this wouldn't be the end of it, and she wished she hadn't been quite so nasty to them.

6

Ginger stood outside the cabin, chewing her gum and waiting for Grandfather to take her to dinner at the Ahwahnee Hotel.

A Stellar's jay squawked from the cedar trees that overshadowed the cabin.

"Squawk, yourself," she called back at the bird.

When he didn't reply, she smoothed the skirt of her new white dress with the green swirls. Gram had made a matching jacket for it and appliquéd a comical green cat on the left side. "Bet you're scared of the cat," she said to the jay, who squawked again.

Berkie and her family had already gone to the cafeteria for dinner, and Ginger thought she'd rather be outside in the forest talking with a squawky bird than waiting in the cabin.

Wandering along, she heard the other cabin door close. She turned, expecting to see Grandfather, but it was Todd.

He rolled his wheelchair out. "You talk to yourself?"

Embarrassed, she said, "I was talking back at that Stellar's jay up there in the tree."

Todd wheeled down the deck's ramp, then glanced up at the huge cedars. "I don't see any bird."

"That doesn't mean there's not one there!" she snapped.

"No, I guess not. I don't have a picture of a jay yet." As usual, he wore his camera around his neck.

"Oh," Ginger said and gave her gum a loud crack. Why did she let her temper get the better of her!

She decided to look at the forest and not say anything for a while. When finally she let her eyes drift past Todd, she noticed he was all dressed up in tan pants, a white shirt, and a tweedy tan sports coat.

"Are you going somewhere special, too?" she asked.

"To the Ahwahnee Hotel for dinner with Grandfather."

"But I'm going there with him," she objected.

Todd's blue-green eyes turned to hers. "We *both* are."

She chewed her gum hard. "Since when?"

"Since he asked me," Todd replied. "Why do you think the van's still parked here?"

"I guess I hadn't thought about it," she admitted.

Closer to Todd now, she saw that the scrapes on his forehead still hadn't healed. She wanted to apologize again, but the way he was looking at her, it wouldn't do any good. "Well, then, I guess you're going, too."

She turned away and wandered along the forested path for a way. *Lord,* she prayed, *help me to be kind to Todd. He sure doesn't make it easy.*

She'd no more than turned back than she saw Kyle and Curt arriving at their cabin, still in their black bathing suits.

"Hey-hey, it's the crazy redhead!" Curt yelled. "Where you going?"

Ginger ignored them and looked up at the cedar trees for the jay.

Kyle called out so loudly that anyone around could hear, "WHERE YOU GOIN' WITH THAT CRIP?"

Crip? Ginger's mind echoed, appalled. *What he meant was cripple!*

She ignored that part of it. But ignoring them entirely hadn't worked, so she said as kindly as possible, "We're going out for dinner to the Ahwahnee Hotel."

"Oh, yeah?" Kyle shot back. "Well, ain't you somethin'?"

She didn't answer, hoping they'd go into their cabin and forget about them.

Instead, Curt yelled over, "Is that crip your brother?"

Ginger gave him a withering look. "It's unkind for you to talk like that."

Curt asked in a phony voice, "Talk like what?"

"Never mind!" Ginger wished she hadn't said a word.

"CRIP, CRIP, CRIP, CRIPPLE!" Curt yelled at Todd.

71

Kyle yelled it with him, "*CRIP, CRIP, CRIP, CRIP-PLE!*"

"He may be in a wheelchair," she yelled back at them, "but he isn't a jerk like you two!"

"Who you callin' a jerk?" Kyle asked.

Just then Grandfather Gabriel came out of the cabin. "What's all of this about?" he asked.

"Nothing good," Ginger answered, clenching her jaw shut.

She noticed that Todd's jaw was set with anger, too. Probably it wasn't the first time he'd had to put up with that kind of talk. When she glanced back toward the boys, they were disappearing into their cabin. *Good riddance!* she thought.

Grandfather locked the cabin door. "Did you lock your side?" he asked Ginger.

She nodded.

"What were those boys saying?" he asked her.

"They were nasty to Todd," she answered. "They bugged Berkie and me at the pool this afternoon, too. Probably because they don't know how to swim."

Todd said, "They're just jerks."

Grandfather drew a breath. "That doesn't sound very charitable."

Ginger still felt mad. "The ranger told us this morning that people come here on vacation, but they bring their problems with them, and those two boys sure must have problems!"

"Perhaps they feel unloved," Grandfather suggested.

Ginger stared down at her new white sandals. The

evening sure hadn't gotten off to a good start.

Grandfather continued, "It's true that people bring their problems along, but I can't remember nasty people here years ago. Maybe I tend to hold onto the good memories." He opened the back of the van for Todd to get in and pushed the button to bring down the hydraulic lift.

Todd was busy getting his wheelchair on the lift, and Grandfather said to Ginger, "I felt as if the two of you should get to know each other better. I hope you're not slighted by my bringing Todd on our date."

"It's okay." She gave her gum a loud crack and headed for the van's front passenger seat. As if it weren't bad enough for her to have tipped Todd over the hillside in his wheelchair, now she had to share her special dinner with Grandfather with him.

After Grandfather got Todd settled, he climbed onto the front seat. He stuck the key into the ignition, and Ginger found herself watching him start the van. Once the motor was running, he pulled off the emergency brake, then moved the gearshift. When they'd backed out onto the drive, he moved the gearshift again and stepped on the gas.

He grinned at her. "You taking up driving?"

"Sure, when I'm sixteen. It's only five years away."

From behind her Todd gave a laugh. "One thing those boys said was right. She's a crazy redhead!"

"Never mind!" Ginger snapped.

Grandfather said quietly, "I'd hoped we might have a pleasant evening."

Ginger grabbed a deep breath. "Me, too."

Grandfather said, "Let's take the apostle Paul's advice. You know, whatsoever things are noble, right, pure, lovely . . . set your mind on those things."

Ginger decided that's what she'd do.

As they drove to the Ahwahnee Hotel, Grandfather kept the conversation on the sights all around them. There were deer among the blooming wildflowers in the meadow, and he asked Todd, "Do you want to stop to take a picture?"

"No, thanks," Todd replied from behind Ginger, where his wheelchair attached to the van's floor. "I have plenty of deer-in-the-meadow pictures. I'd like to get some pictures by the hotel, though. Maybe inside, too. One of the men at the convalescent home said he'd stayed there a long time ago."

Grandfather told Ginger, "Todd was taking pictures this morning, but we ran out of film at the Ahwahnee. Unfortunately, their gift shop was out of the kind he needs."

They passed the clinic in an uncomfortable silence. At least Todd didn't want to stop for a picture of it! Just seeing it reminded her of his sliding down the hillside in his wheelchair. It *was* her fault, no matter what the others said.

"Almost there," Grandfather said as they pulled into the hotel's driveway. He stopped the van in front of the massive pine log and rock building, whose rocks were as gray as Half Dome, the mountain towering just behind it.

"Wow!" Ginger said. "It's nothing like I expected." She noticed that the hotel's wooden shutters were painted bright turquoise, suiting its Indian name.

"It's certainly a long cry from what the Indian people of Ahwahnee lived in," Grandfather observed.

Ginger remembered the Indian village. "They lived in buildings that looked like bark teepees."

Behind her Todd murmured, "Well, aren't you smart?"

She felt her temper rising again, then realized it was the kind of quip Joshua, her stepbrother, would make. Instead of snapping back, she turned and gave him a fast grin.

Beside her, she was glad to see Grandfather smile.

When they pulled up in front of the hotel, Grandfather said, "We'll use valet service tonight and pretend we're royalty."

One of the green-vested valets opened her door, but Ginger climbed out by herself. "Thank you," she remembered to say. She felt a little stupid, as if she couldn't open the door herself . . . maybe the way Todd felt at times, too?

Once his wheelchair was settled on the ground, Todd looked at the scenery. "I'd like to get some pictures that show the parklike grounds. Let's go over to the stream there."

Grandfather glanced at his watch. "I think we just have time enough before dinner."

Ginger asked him, "Could we get copies of some of the slides so I could show Mom and the rest of the

75

family? I could pay for them. I have some money."

"Why don't you ask Todd?" Grandfather suggested.

She glanced at Todd and made herself ask, "Could I?"

"Sure," he answered, pleased. When he took pictures, even back at Happy Isles, he really seemed exciting and alive, just like Berkie said he'd been before the accident. Ginger liked this Todd a lot better.

After he'd taken pictures of the burbling stream, they headed back to the hotel, then across its covered veranda. Log benches lined the walkway, and the outside walls were of rough wood and logs painted with Indian markings.

Ginger said, "Mom would like a postcard of this, too. What she'd really like to do is to come here and paint everything on canvas."

"Is your mom an artist?" Todd asked.

"She's trying to be," Ginger answered. Since he sounded interested, she added, "You know, she takes classes and paints a lot of pictures. She's going to have three of them on exhibit at the county fair."

Todd said, "I'm going to have some photographs on exhibit at our fair, too."

"I didn't know that," Ginger said.

"Todd's had some of his pictures printed in their local newspaper, too," Grandfather told Ginger.

Ginger eyed Todd with a new appreciation and found him smiling a little at her. "Hey, that's all right!"

"We'll hit the gift shop for postcards after dinner," Grandfather said. "Right now we'd better hurry along if we don't want to lose our reservation."

Inside, Todd snapped pictures of the old-fashioned three-story lounge. The windows were three stories tall, too, and looked out at the wonderful views.

Ginger said, "Look at those fireplaces!"

"It's said that thirty people can stand in them at the same time," Grandfather replied.

"Mom would like to paint this room, too." It was furnished with antiques and enormous black chandeliers, and Indian design rugs hung on the walls.

They headed for the dining room and, near the entrance, a black-suited man played beautiful music on a grand piano.

The maitre d', who stood at the door, asked their name.

"Gabriel," Grandfather said.

"Follow me, please," the maitre d' said with dignity.

Ginger followed him on a red carpet through the middle of elegantly set tables in the high-ceilinged dining room. It was a sight to behold: chandeliers alight with candles, great peeled logs holding up the ceiling, and tall windows that looked out at the mountains.

She felt people watching them and decided they must be a sight to behold, too: a redheaded girl with wild curls, a boy in a wheelchair, and a handsome silvery-haired grandfather.

Finally she was seated without having tripped or caused any disasters. She remembered to say, "Thank you" and was glad for Grandfather's smile of approval.

A busboy helped with Todd's wheelchair, and in no

time they were settled at the round table. Like the other tables, it had a pink tablecloth, a lighted candle, water goblets, and an impressive lineup of silverware.

Their waiter arrived to present their menus, and Ginger opened hers, trying to decide what to order.

Todd warned Grandfather, "It's going to be expensive."

Grandfather nodded, smiling a little. "Don't worry about that. One benefit of being retired is my having time to write. I just sold an article on joy to *Sunday Digest*, so let's enjoy it. We may never have a chance to eat here again."

Ginger wondered if Todd ever felt joy in his heart like she did since she'd become a Christian. The only glimpse she'd seen of any joy was when he was taking pictures. She grinned at Todd. "Grandfather is trying to get us 'cultured.' "

Todd grinned a little himself, and Grandfather laughed.

"It's nice to see people dressed up for a change, even at Yosemite, isn't it?" Grandfather remarked.

"It makes you feel more grown up," Ginger allowed. "And it reminds us to use good manners."

"We can all use more of that," Grandfather said.

Things were going better, Ginger thought, and set her mind firmly on the menu. She decided on *gazpacho*, a spicy cold soup that Mom had made last summer, and on a chicken dish that sounded foreign, too.

When they all sat back, Ginger tried to fill the

silence. "Why do you want to climb a mountain?" she asked Todd.

"I didn't say I'd go. I'm only here to see if I really want to climb."

"Oh," she answered and was glad to see the busboy arrive to serve the ice water. From now on, she'd let the piano music fill any silences. Maybe that's what the music was for.

Grandfather began to talk about what Yosemite was like years ago when he'd visited, and Ginger half-listened and half-watched the busboys and waiters carry trays full of dishes over their heads with one hand. Mom would say they did it with a flair, Ginger thought. Mom and Grant would have a good time staying in a cabin at Yosemite. So would Joshua and Lilabet. But her own dad would probably only like it if he could stay at the Ahwahnee because it was impressive. And maybe he'd like to climb mountains.

After their rolls were served, Grandfather said grace with the piano music floating around his words like a beautiful sunrise. When they all looked up again, he remarked, "I've been thinking about those boys in the next cabin. Ginger, didn't you say they don't know how to swim?"

"I don't know for sure," she answered. "But when they wouldn't stop bugging Berkie and me at the pool, I finally said, 'What's wrong with you two? Don't you know how to swim?' They looked like I'd hit right on the truth, and then they left."

Todd shot a skeptical glance at her. "What are you,

some kind of a psychiatrist?"

"Never mind!"

"Hmmmm," Grandfather said, ignoring them. "I wonder where they're from. Maybe we can help."

Ginger nodded. "I felt bad after I'd said that, but I didn't know what to do then."

"What do you think we should do?" Grandfather asked.

She felt her face get red. "Pray for them, I guess." It was the first time she'd even thought of it.

"There's no guessing about it," her grandfather replied as he got out his blue plastic pillbox and took out a pill. "We should especially pray for troublesome people. Usually they're that way because they need love."

The waiter brought their soup, and Ginger remembered to use the outside spoon on the table for her *gazpacho*. Now, the trick was not to slop it on her new white dress. She pulled the pink napkin on her lap a little higher.

As they ate their dinner with the lovely music filling the beautiful room, she wondered if Kyle and Curt had ever been anywhere this nice for dinner. Probably not.

The sun had already set by the time they'd finished dinner and bought postcards at the gift shop. "Time to get our trusty chariot," Grandfather said as they headed for the lantern-lit veranda of the hotel.

Before long they were in the van and driving out to their cabin again. Ginger said, "I wonder if the rest of them are back at the cabin yet."

"I doubt it," Grandfather said. "They were staying for a ranger talk. I expect we can manage to tuck ourselves in."

"I really had a nice dinner," Ginger said to him. "Thank you. I'm glad I have the postcards, too. When I write them, I'll tell Mom to save them so I can always remember it."

Grandfather patted her arm. "It was my pleasure."

She supposed he was pleased because she and Todd had at least gotten to know each other a little better. Not that it seemed to make much difference to Todd.

They drove past the parking lot and up the road to their cabin. As their headlights shone into the handicapped parking space, Ginger's spine straightened. "Who's that out there?"

"Where?" Grandfather asked.

"Someone ducked around the back of the cabin in the shadows!" she said. "I saw them for sure."

From behind her, Todd said, "I didn't see anyone."

She still felt scared as she peered out into the darkness. "Well, I did!"

"Maybe it was those boys from the next cabin," Todd said.

Ginger drew a deep breath. "I wouldn't be surprised."

When Grandfather unlocked the doors, Ginger snapped on the light on her side of the cabin and hurried in. Drawers and clothes were thrown all over the room. "Someone was here!" she shouted. "Someone sure was here!"

The "boys' side" was a shambles, too, and their bathroom window was broken. Shattered glass lay everywhere.

Minutes later, Berkie, Aunt Jennie, and Uncle Charlie arrived. "What happened?" they asked with amazement.

"A break-in," Grandfather said.

When they'd all cleaned up the mess and taken stock, they realized nothing was missing.

Uncle Charlie gave a rueful laugh. "We didn't bring anything worth stealing except our money and Todd's camera, and we carried those with us. We'd better all simmer down. I'll report it to the rangers right now."

"If they ask about suspicious characters," Todd said, "tell them about those kids in the next cabin."

Uncle Charlie said, "Only if you think I should."

"I think so," Todd said.

Ginger nodded. "But all we know is they're nasty."

"That's not much to tell the rangers," Uncle Charlie said.

Grandfather suggested, "The best thing to do is to pray for whoever broke in. Let's do that now."

They all bowed their heads, and Grandfather said, "Heavenly Father, You have given us so much for which to be grateful, especially when we see the beauty of Your creation at a place like Yosemite. We praise You and thank You for that. You tell us to give thanks in spite of all things, so we give thanks in spite of this break-in. We ask that You would turn it into a blessing to Your glory, whether now or in years to come. It may seem impossible to us, but everything is possible with You. We pray this in Christ's powerful name. Amen."

It seemed forever before the rangers came and then finally left. They were sorry as could be about the break-in, but there was little they could do except watch for the culprits and call the maintenance department to board up the broken bathroom window.

As Ginger settled into bed, she was grateful that nothing was stolen and that they were all safe together. When they turned out the cabin light, she realized she was really growing to love Berkie and Aunt Jennie and Uncle Charlie.

As for Todd—she felt sorry for him sometimes, like when those boys had been so nasty . . . but she couldn't say that she loved him. If that's what Grandfather had hoped to accomplish by taking both of them to dinner, it hadn't worked at all. Asking for kindness toward her stepcousin hadn't been enough. *God*, she prayed, *give me Your love for Todd.*

7

The next morning when Ginger stepped outside, she quickly looked at the next cabin. It was close enough that she could see the plaid draperies were partially open, but far enough away that she couldn't see anyone inside. She chewed her gum hard, wondering if those boys were the ones who had broken into their cabin.

As she stood there, a skinny woman with black hair stepped out the door with a beer can in her hand. She plopped down on the edge of their deck and took a drink, then gave Ginger what looked like a mean look. Just then a man came out to join her. He shot a nasty look at Ginger, too.

Ginger turned away, clenching her fists, and sat down on the wood deck of her cabin. A good thing they were far away or she might say something she'd regret.

Berkie opened the cabin door behind her. "Mom said we could go now so we can get to the rafts early. I brought some granola bars and bananas for our breakfast."

Ginger rose to her feet. "Good." She added under her breath, "Don't look now, but I think the boys' parents are out on their deck."

Berkie waited until they'd passed by some bushes, then glanced over. "They're staring daggers at us."

"I don't know why," Ginger said, opening the wrapper of her granola bar. "We're the ones whose cabin was broken into!"

Berkie shrugged. "Probably the boys made up something mean about us."

"Probably," Ginger decided. "They're just the type who would. What are we going to say if we see them today?"

"I don't know," her cousin replied. "Maybe they aren't even the ones who broke into our cabin." She let out a discouraged breath. "It could be thousands of people here at Yosemite. Anyhow, Dad reported it."

"Let's not even think about it," Ginger said. "It's such a nice morning, I don't want them or anybody else to ruin our day. Grandfather would say we should keep our minds on whatsoever is good and noble and lovely—"

"He's right about that," Berkie replied.

A woodpecker rat-a-tat-tatted on a tree nearby, but

they couldn't see him. Berkie said, "You must be glad to have Grandfather living so close by."

"You're right about that!" Ginger said, feeling better.

They both wore white shorts and T-shirts, and Berkie had lent Ginger an extra white hair bow. With the sunshine streaming through the forest, it did seem that everything was fresh and new. Ginger was *not* going to think about those boys again!

As she peeled her banana she said, "If Lilabet were here, she'd tell you she got her yellow hair from eating bananas."

Berkie laughed. "It must be fun to have a little sister."

"Sometimes," Ginger admitted. "Sometimes not. But I like her a lot now."

"Todd used to be so much fun," Berkie said as they headed toward the tram stop. "Even after the accident, he wasn't as awful as he's been this week."

"I guess it's hard for him to decide about climbing a mountain when he's in a wheelchair," Ginger replied.

Berkie nodded. "I shouldn't have mentioned it. It's just that it's always on my mind now that we're here, and I don't want to say anything to him. It has to be his decision."

Ginger nodded. "I can imagine how grouchy Joshua would be if it happened to him. And I don't even want to think how awful I'd be, if it happened to me."

"Look—" Berkie said. "There's Grandfather now."

"Sure enough."

He drove his white Plymouth over alongside the road and waited for them.

When Ginger opened the door, he asked, "Would you young ladies like a ride to the raft rental place?"

"We're not supposed to ride with strangers," Ginger teased.

They all laughed, and she and Berkie piled into the car.

"Did you eat breakfast?" Ginger asked him.

"I hung around the cabin while the maintenance men fixed our bathroom window," he explained.

"At least it's fixed," Ginger said. She didn't like remembering that someone had gone through all of her stuff.

"Then I gave the local pastor a call," Grandfather continued, "and I'm invited to breakfast with him."

"All right!" she said. Grandfather made friends fast, and it didn't surprise her at all.

Before long, they pulled up near the raft rental place at Curry Village. "Here you are, ladies," Grandfather said. "I might just stop by later to see if you need a ride back to the cabin. If I'm not here, you can always take the tram." He added, "I'm on the loose today."

Berkie put a hand over her mouth, muffling a laugh.

"What's so amusing?" Grandfather asked, smiling himself.

Berkie's cheeks had turned a little pink. "It sounds funny to hear a minister say he's on the loose."

Grandfather said, "It's funnier yet to hear what people think a minister should or shouldn't say. So many forget that we're simply people like others, too."

"I guess so," Berkie replied. "I always think that ministers are . . . you know, special to God."

"You're just as special to Him," he answered. "So are Ginger and Todd and your parents. Every one of us is special to Him. So special that God wants each of us to have a ministry."

"That's what our Sunday school teacher told us, too," Berkie answered.

Ginger said, "Maybe your ministry will come through working as a nurse or a doctor."

Berkie raised her brows, wondering. "Maybe. Maybe I can even be a medical missionary. What about you?"

Ginger shook her head. "I don't know. I wonder lots of times, but I still don't know."

Grandfather assured her, "God will let you know when the time comes. He's already used you in some interesting ways, and I wouldn't be surprised if you're not used often if you stay close to Him."

"That's the trouble," Ginger admitted. "I forget to stay as close as I should."

"Don't we all?" Grandfather asked. "Don't we all?"

He drove them into Camp Curry and dropped them off near the raft rental shop. When they climbed out of the car, he said a hearty, "Good rafting!"

"Good breakfasting!" Ginger replied with a grin and slammed the car door. "Thanks for the ride!"

She and Berkie waved to him, then made their way toward the river.

"He's wonderful, isn't he?" Berkie said.

Ginger nodded and hoped he'd remember his breakfast pill.

At the shop, the girls decided on a dark red raft, then carried it down to the nearby river. Attendants were ready to help them and to make sure that they put on their life jackets. In no time at all, Ginger and Berkie were sitting on either side of the raft and paddling out onto the river with their oars.

"Just look ahead at those kids on inner tubes!" Ginger said. Her body gave a shiver as she thought about sitting in the cold water. "You'd think they'd freeze."

"You know it!" Berkie, who'd rafted on rivers before, turned their raft with her oar so they'd float downriver with the water's current.

As their raft moved down the middle of the river, the mountains and forests surrounding Yosemite Valley were not only all around them, but were reflected on the clear green water. "Isn't it beautiful here?" Ginger said as they floated along. "It's like being in a wonderful dream."

Berkie nodded.

They floated along in silence for a while. "Look," Berkie said, pointing to nearby fishermen, "someone's caught a fish."

Sure enough, a man was hauling a fish from the water.

"Wonder if there are any fish under us?" Ginger asked apprehensively.

"Maybe sharks!" Berkie joked.

As they floated on, there were picnickers finishing breakfast and a few early sunbathers, but most of them were quiet.

Farther along, bushes lined the riverbanks and red-winged blackbirds flew about. A hush filled the air. Rafting was an especially peaceful way to see the meadows and forests and mountains, Ginger decided.

After a while, though, they heard kids' voices ahead. They drifted around a bend in the river, and Ginger raised a hand to shield the sun from her eyes. "Ufffff! I can't believe it! I think it's those boys again!"

Berkie squinted, too. "It sure looks like them!"

The boys were yelling and pushing each other around wildly in their big, black inner tubes.

"We don't want to catch up with them!" Ginger said.

"We'll just have to dawdle along closer to the banks whenever we can to stay out of the main current," Berkie replied.

They paddled toward the bank to get out of sight, but at the last moment, Kyle glanced at them.

Ginger's throat tightened, and she paddled faster. "I think they saw us!"

Berkie pulled harder for the shore. "We'll have to wait here for a while. There's no way we can paddle back upriver."

They waited near the shore for a long time. Finally, Ginger said, "We can't wait forever. Let's go on again."

Moments later, they came around the forested bend in the river. The boys yelled, then paddled wildly with their arms toward the girls. "I knew it was you two!" Kyle shouted.

"We've got to get in the middle of the river!" Berkie yelled to Ginger. "Paddle as fast as you can!"

The current grew swifter, and their raft moved rapidly.

"We're gonna dunk you girls!" Curt yelled, churning up the water as he and his brother came at them in the inner tubes.

Paddling with all of her might, Ginger shouted, "You leave us alone!" She stuck her oar out at Kyle's inner tube and pushed it away, then pushed at Curt's, too. "Faster, faster!" she cried out to Berkie.

"I'm paddling as fast as I can!" Berkie yelled.

The boys came at them with their inner tubes again, water thrashing and splashing wildly around them. This time when Ginger pushed at their inner tubes, they grabbed for her oar.

"Yii! Stop that!" She almost tipped out of the raft and jerked the oar back. "You shouldn't even be out here where it's deep if you can't swim!"

They must have realized how far out in the the river they were because they backed off a little, and the raft began to outdistance them.

"Paddle, Ginger!" Berkie yelled. "Paddle hard!"

Ginger's arms ached as she paddled on. Slowly but surely, the boys dropped back.

"Whew!" she said, easing off. She glanced upriver again. "It looks like they're going to the riverbank."

"Thank goodness!" Berkie said with relief. "I think

you're right. They don't know how to swim."

The rest of the raft trip was better, and they began to enjoy the scenery again. An hour later, when they neared El Capitán, lots of mountaineers were inching up its sheer cliff.

Berkie remarked, "That's what Todd would probably like to do, if he weren't in a wheelchair."

Ginger nodded. "Yeah. I bet he would."

"He took pictures of the climbers yesterday for us to show at the convalescent home," Berkie said.

Ginger wondered if seeing others climb made him feel better or worse. "He *has* to go on that "Go for It" climb!"

"I know it," Berkie answered. "He really does. And he only has two more days to decide!"

At the El Capitan picnic area, raft trip attendants waited to help them off the rafts and direct them to the bus that would take them back to Camp Curry.

"It was a neat trip," Ginger said, "Except for the boys."

"Yeah," Berkie replied. "But I don't think we've seen the last of them yet."

Grandfather drove up just as they climbed off the raft shuttle bus, and they all decided to have hamburgers on the Meadow Deck again. "What are you girls going to do this afternoon?" he asked.

"We thought we'd hike to the Lodge, then maybe swim again," Ginger said. "I just hope those boys from the next cabin aren't at the pool today! You'll never believe it, but they were out on the river in inner tubes, trying to drown us!"

"I'm glad you survived," Grandfather said.

"Just barely!" Berkie returned.

After Ginger told how they'd escaped, she added, "I'll bet they're madder than ever at us."

"It'd probably be a good idea for me to talk to them," Grandfather remarked thoughtfully. "Maybe an opportunity will present itself."

That afternoon there was no sign of Kyle and Curt at the pool, nor anywhere else. A sudden storm hit and, even when Ginger and Berkie hurried back to the cabin, the boys were nowhere to be seen.

"Maybe they've gone home," Ginger said hopefully as they came in the door.

Todd and Grandfather were already inside, and Todd sounded angry. "You mean the neighborhood nasties? That would be too good to be true."

"Why?" Ginger asked, a little embarrassed to see Todd sitting on his bed with his limp legs lying in front of him. "Did you see them today?"

"Yeah," he said. "I don't want to talk about it."

Ginger was sure they'd yelled "Crip-crip-crip-cripple!" at him again. In a way, it was even worse than her letting Todd and his wheelchair tilt over and slide down the hill.

Grandfather said, "How about a game of Scrabble while we wait for the rain to stop?"

"All right! Good idea!" Todd agreed, his mood changing right away.

"Yeah," Berkie said, "But Todd will probably win, as usual. He's the kind of a player who loves to get Qs, Js, and Xs, and anything else that's hard to get rid of!"

"They're a challenge," Todd said.

"And you do like challenges!" Berkie answered.

"Some," Todd answered with a grin.

Ginger decided he wasn't thinking of the "Go for It" climb at the moment. "I'm not so good at Scrabble yet," she admitted. "I just learned how to play when Mom and Grant got married."

Grandfather gave a laugh. "You're learning too fast to suit me. Last time we played, you beat Joshua and me!"

"That was the only time, though!" Ginger protested. "I couldn't believe it myself."

"Let's play on my bed," Berkie suggested, "since the girls' side of the cabin is so much neater than the boys'."

Todd gave a laugh and scooted over to get from his bed into his wheelchair. "I won't argue with that!"

They all settled on and around Berkie's bed. "Let Todd turn over the letters," she said when Grandfather opened the Scrabble box. "Todd just flips them, and they're all upside down. He's the family expert at that, too."

Sure enough, he closed the box and flipped it so perfectly that only two letters were wrong side up. "Oops!" he said, "I'm losing my touch."

They laughed, and Berkie warned Ginger, "You're sitting on the wrong side of Todd. He never opens spaces for the person behind him."

Ginger said, "Yeah, well, I'll just do my best."

Todd gave her a surprised but approving look.

They each chose a wooden letter to see who would play first, and Grandfather got a B, the lowest. When they all had their letters, Grandfather put down his first word, BUSTLE. "Meaning 'to hurry,' of course," he joked.

He'd no more than settled the letters on the board than Todd used the E to spell out EQUINOX—using up six of his letters and getting all kinds of extra scores.

"Oh, Todd-o!" Berkie groaned. She turned to Ginger. "Didn't I warn you? Look, he's used a Q and an X first thing off. He's like that with computers and math, too. It's awfully discouraging to have such a whiz for a brother."

"Oh, come on, Berk-o!" Todd protested, trying not to look pleased. "You're not so bad at art and writing reports and that kind of stuff. You'll just never beat me at Scrabble!"

Ginger smiled, glad to see how much they liked each other.

And, as far as Todd blocking open spaces so she couldn't put down good words, he wasn't so hard on her after all. When they'd finished the game—with Todd winning, of course—she decided that she was beginning to like him, just a little.

Aunt Jennie and Uncle Charlie returned right after the rain stopped. "Guess it's the cafeteria for dinner," Uncle Charlie said. "It's too wet to cook on the grill."

After dinner, though, it was dry enough to sit outside and enjoy a ranger slide program about Yosemite. The sky had cleared, and when the program ended, they took their time getting back. It seemed that the stars were closer and thicker than ever in the night sky. The Milky Way was a river of light, and Uncle Charlie pointed out the Big Dipper and the North Star and Scorpio and Sagittarius.

"A shooting star!" Grandfather said. "Make a wish!"

Ginger wished that Todd would do the "Go for It" climb.

As they moved on, they decided on tomorrow's plans. It was Sunday, so they'd attend the church service at the Lower River Campground, then have a late lunch at the Wawona Hotel. After that, they'd visit the Pioneer Yosemite History Center and then—maybe— the base camp for Todd's "Go for It" climb.

When they arrived at their cabin, the lights over both doors were out.

"I'm certain I turned on the one over the girls' door," Aunt Jennie said with concern.

"I know I left ours on, too," Uncle Charlie added.

Ginger remembered the mess they'd walked into last night, and swallowed hard. Probably the others remembered, too.

Uncle Charlie and Grandfather had flashlights, so they could find their way up the deck without breaking their necks. Grandfather unlocked the door on the boys' side, then turned on the inside overhead light. "It looks fine," he said.

Aunt Jennie went through the connecting door and turned on the light. "It seems fine here . . . except the door lock looks peculiar, like it was jimmied open."

Todd wheeled through in his wheelchair, heading for the chest of drawers. "My camera's gone!"

"Are you sure?" Uncle Charlie asked.

Todd clenched his fists. "I thought it'd be safe, since they didn't find anything here last night!"

Ginger knew without asking, it was a *very* good camera. And taking pictures was the one thing that Todd really enjoyed. A stolen camera was the last thing he needed right now.

8

When Ginger stepped out of the cabin the next morning, the beauty of trees and mountains made her feel a little better about Todd's missing camera. A good thing it was Sunday, she decided. No matter what happened in life, going to church and knowing that God loved them always helped.

She glanced at the next cabin. To her amazement, there was Grandfather Gabriel on the nearby path talking to Kyle and Curt. Was he telling them to return the camera? she wondered. Maybe even demanding it? Not that she could imagine Grandfather demanding anything.

Finally he turned to leave, and the boys smiled at him. If he'd asked for the camera back, they sure hadn't given it.

"Good morning, Ginger," Grandfather said as he approached.

"Good morning . . . Did you ask them about Todd's camera?"

His silvery hair shone in the sunlight, and his kindly blue eyes sparkled as he shook his head. "No, no, I didn't. Are you certain they took it?"

"No," she admitted. "I guess not. What were you talking about then?"

He gave a laugh. "Since you've asked so directly, I suppose I can tell you. But you have to keep it to yourself."

"Okay, I promise."

"I wanted to know where they're from," Grandfather said. "I've offered to sponsor YMCA swimming lessons for them."

"You're going to pay for their swimming lessons?"

"Not so loud," Grandfather warned. "But, yes, that's what I told them I'd do."

"Why would you do that?" she asked.

"When we see a need that we can fill, I believe the Lord would like us to take care of it, even if the person is a stranger," Grandfather said.

"What did they say?"

Grandfather grinned. "At first, they were just as astonished as you. I suspect they've never had anyone do something like that for them."

"Are they going to take the swimming lessons?"

"It took some talking to convince them. I told them it would give me a lot of pleasure, and that's what finally made them accept. I suppose they think I'm a little peculiar."

"I guess so!" Ginger said. It was peculiar, all right.

Later, when they rode the tram to the church service at the Lower River Campground's amphitheater, Ginger thought about it all again. *Lord,* she prayed, *let Grandfather's kindness make a difference in those boys.*

The amphitheater didn't look at all like a church, she decided when they arrived. There was only a raised log platform with a wooden roof and a back wall. Rows of benches and tree stumps provided seating in front of the platform. But the towering pine and cedar trees around them made it a beautiful place anyhow.

As they headed for the benches, Grandfather told Ginger and Berkie, "Seminary and college students perform most of the services in national parks. It's good training for them and a blessing to the people who attend the services."

Most of those arriving wore jeans or denim skirts like hers, so it was easy to tell who the students were— the young men wore neckties and the girls wore casual dresses.

"They look younger than the people in charge of our church," Ginger noted.

Grandfather chuckled. "That they are."

A pretty blonde college girl handed her a program. "Good morning," she said, but Ginger just said, "Thanks."

"Let's sit up front," Grandfather suggested. "Most people don't like to, so we'll take advantage of their

100

reluctance and encourage others to sit closer, all in one swoop."

Uncle Charlie said, "They're the best seats in the house anyhow. What's more, you're not distracted by the fidgeters."

Berkie teased Ginger. "Are you a fidgeter?"

Ginger grinned. "Not too much. Grant won't let us. He says it disturbs everyone else."

They sat on a front row bench: Grandfather, Ginger, Berkie, Aunt Jennie, and Uncle Charlie, with Todd sitting in his wheelchair on the outside edge.

Ginger studied her program with the picture of a great snowcapped mountain. Above in the blue sky was printed Psalm 125:1: "Those who trust in the Lord are like Mount Zion, which can never be shaken, never be moved." That's when she did best, she decided—when she really trusted God.

After a while, two young men strummed praise songs on their guitars while people settled on the benches and tree trunks. Before long, a sandy-haired young man wearing a gray suit with a red necktie stepped up on the stage. "This is the day that the Lord has made. Let us rejoice and be glad in it!" he pronounced. "Let us worship the Creator of this beautiful place we call Yosemite!"

He had nice dimples like Mom, Ginger thought, and he had what Grandfather called a loving spirit. She decided on the spot that she liked him.

They all bowed their heads, and he asked God to bless them and the service. Then they all stood and sang, "Joyful, joyful, we adore Thee, God of glory, Lord of love . . . hearts unfold like flowers before Thee. . . ."

Ginger's heart did feel like a flower unfolding to God. She loved the joyous music and words, especially "Thou our Father, Christ our Brother, All who live in love are Thine, Teach us how to love each other, Lift us to the Joy divine."

She glanced at Todd and was glad to see that he was singing out, too.

The sermon was about worshiping God instead of what He'd created, even if it was full of beautiful forests, waterfalls, and mountains like Yosemite. After the offering and a prayer of thanksgiving, they sang, "How Great Thou Art."

Ginger glanced at Todd when they sang out, "When I look down from lofty mountain grandeur." He'd have to decide tomorrow if he was going to climb a mountain in his wheelchair with the "Go for It" group, or not.

After the benediction, they headed back for the tram. Today they'd drive to the Wawona Hotel for a late lunch, then visit the Pioneer Yosemite History Center, and last—if Todd wanted to—visit the Summit Adventure base camp.

When they arrived back at the cabin, Ginger and Berkie got in the front seat of Grandfather's car, since they wouldn't all fit in the van. They drove out of Yosemite the same way they'd driven in. This time, though, Ginger had someone to hold her breath with all through the long tunnel.

"Whew! We did it!" Berkie exclaimed as they came out into the sunlight again.

"Yea!" Ginger said, taking another deep breath.

As they wound along the curving road through the forest, Grandfather said, "The Wawona is one of the oldest hotels still operating in California. Would you believe it was once a stagecoach stop?"

When they arrived, Ginger believed it. The two-story Hotel Wawona stood in a clearing in the forest. Except for its bright green golf course across the road, the long white hotel looked like just the place for a stagecoach to stop years ago. It wasn't as impressive as the Ahwahnee Hotel standing right in front of Half Dome, but it was just as interesting in an old-fashioned way.

"I can imagine horses and a stagecoach driving up," she said. "It's sure not like our hotels at home."

"No, that it isn't," Grandfather agreed.

After they parked, he escorted her and Berkie and Aunt Jennie up the flight of steps to the hotel's long front porch, while Uncle Charlie went around back with Todd to go up a wheelchair ramp. In the dining room, Ginger sat down at the table between Berkie and Grandfather, and Aunt Jennie settled across from her.

Todd was frowning a little when he wheeled in with his father. When they settled at the table, Ginger said, "It's too bad there isn't a front handicapped ramp."

Todd shot her an angry look and snapped, "I might be disabled, but I am *not* handicapped!"

She opened her mouth to apologize, but he was so

mad he didn't stop. "A handicap is caused by barriers or obstacles that keep people with physical disabilities from doing daily tasks," he said. "It's *places* and *people* who handicap me!"

Probably people like me! Ginger thought and swallowed uncomfortably. "I—I'd never thought of it like that."

Uncle Charlie explained, "Todd prefers to be called disabled if you're going to mention his disability."

"I'm sorry!" Ginger said, heartsick. "I'm really sorry!" As if things weren't bad enough for him without her making them worse!

He gave her another angry look, but said nothing.

Grandfather said, "I'm sure that Todd will find it in his heart to forgive you. I know that all of us at this table have loving hearts and mean well. Let's say grace now."

Grandfather's prayer seemed to help matters a little, and their lunch helped, too. Not that Todd had much to say. By dessert—slices of hot apple pie with ice cream—Todd seemed a little less angry.

After lunch, they drove to the nearby Pioneer Yosemite History Center. There were old-fashioned horse-drawn buggies and wagons, and even a big covered bridge over a stream. In the rustic village, the villagers—who were really actors—wore pioneer clothes as they went about their work.

Ginger explored the wooden cabins, the jail, and the other buildings with Berkie, and tried to keep her distance from Todd. She overhead Grandfather tell him, "I'll buy you slides of this for your program at the convalescent home." That was reminder enough that Todd no longer had his camera.

Uncle Charlie asked, "How would you girls like to ride in the horse-drawn wagon?"

"Yeah!" Berkie answered, and it sounded like a good idea to Ginger, too.

The driver, dressed like a cowboy, helped them up into a seat, then took up the reins to the four chestnut horses. "Gid-up, boys!" he yelled out at them, and the horses clip-clopped off.

It was fun to bounce along through the forest in the old-fashioned wagon with clouds of dust billowing behind them.

"I expect this is what it felt like to be pioneers here," Berkie remarked.

"I guess so," Ginger agreed.

When their wagon ride ended and the driver helped them down, there was Todd glaring at them.

Berkie said under her breath, "I don't know what we've done wrong."

Ginger shrugged. It seemed as if Todd were getting madder and madder.

After they'd explored the pioneer center, Uncle Charlie said, "Okay, gang, let's go. Todd's decided he wants to talk a bit more to the staff at Summit Adventure."

Ginger and Berkie glanced at each other, then at Todd.

He gave them such a cold look that Ginger was more

glad than ever that they weren't riding in the van with him. Probably he was scared and didn't want them to know—that's why he acted so angry. If only he'd remember what it said above the mountain on the church bulletin: "Those who trust in the Lord are like Mount Zion, which can never be shaken. . . ."

They drove on toward Bass Lake through the forest and mountains. At last Uncle Charlie pulled into a driveway marked "Summit Adventure," and Grandfather drove in behind. An old log building stood at the end of the driveway, and Grandfather parked a few spaces from the van.

Ginger climbed out of the car after Berkie and asked, "Did you see the 'Go for It' video?"

Berkie nodded uneasily, then darted a glance at Todd, who was coming down the van's hydraulic lift in his wheelchair. She said under her breath, "I keep thinking about the man who tipped out of his wheelchair when they got started."

"Yeah," Ginger said, "but he didn't mind. He wanted to go up anyhow, and he did all right, too."

Ginger imagined in her mind's eye the way Todd would climb. First, two men would strap themselves to the front of his wheelchair to pull and two would push from behind. Todd would wear a crash helmet and, as they started climbing the granite domes, he'd probably be as nervous as he looked now.

Berkie said, "The ones on the video were really brave. They wanted the challenge."

Ginger nodded as they made their way toward the

rest of the family. "Most of them were older than Todd is, though. Maybe they were more . . . you know, used to being disabled."

Grandfather was just joining Uncle Charlie and Aunt Jennie as Todd rolled his wheelchair off the van's lift.

Todd glanced about at the base camp, and his chin turned more square than ever. "I don't think I want to talk to the staff after all."

"But we drove all the way here," Uncle Charlie said.

"It would be an incredible adventure," Grandfather said to Todd. "Those five days would be something to remember all of your life."

Aunt Jennie added, "You'd learn to trust more in others and, most of all, in God."

Todd stared up at the log building, then suddenly wheeled his wheelchair around. "I don't want to trust more in others . . . or in God! I'm not going! Let's get out of here!"

9

Driving back to the cabin, Grandfather remarked, "Todd hasn't entirely accepted the fact that he's permanently disabled. He's still set on doing things by himself and in his own way."

Ginger said, "I guess I like to, too."

"It's such a shame for Todd now, though," Grandfather added. "I think there'd be a great spiritual stretch in such a climb. God could use Todd then to touch others' lives."

Berkie added, "Dad thinks if Todd doesn't go he'll be handicapping himself."

Ginger remembered Todd's angry outburst during lunch. "It's *places* and *people* who handicap me!" he'd said. It was probably true, but this time it was just like

Berkie said. Todd was handicapping himself.

I wish I could help, Ginger thought.

When they returned to the cabin, Todd went to bed with a book and refused to eat dinner.

The next morning he was hungry enough to go to breakfast with them, though. Ginger thought he must be starved.

In the cafeteria, she sat a safe distance from him again. After Grandfather said grace, he remembered to take his pill.

Ginger wolfed down her steaming scrambled eggs almost as hungrily as Todd was eating his. She could imagine Mom saying, "Slow down, Ginger! Slow down!"

When they'd almost finished breakfast, she saw Grandfather pop another pill into his mouth and drink it down with his orange juice. Probably just an aspirin, she decided.

"Don't look now," Berkie said, "but there's Kyle and Curt sitting over by the window with their parents!"

Ginger spread blackberry jelly on her English muffin. "I'm not going to look over there at all!"

Later, on the way out of the cafeteria, Berkie said, "I guess Kyle and Curt and their family left already."

"Good!" Ginger said. "I'm praying for them, but I don't care to hear, 'There's that crazy redhead' one more time!"

As they moved on through the crowded cafeteria, she overhead Uncle Charlie tell Grandfather, "We feel it'd be better for Todd to spend the morning with you and Ginger. Would you mind terribly?"

"Not at all," Grandfather answered. "Not at all."

Ginger wasn't sure what she might have answered. It was one thing to pray for difficult people, but another to be with them. She saw Grandfather's eyes close in prayer, then he turned and waited for Aunt Jennie and Todd to catch up.

As he stepped outside beside Todd's wheelchair, Grandfather said, "You know, Todd, you'll be missing pictures of the Ahwahnee Hotel for your slide show. Why don't we go back to their gift shop, and I'll buy you some slides there?"

Todd considered it, then said, "Okay, sure."

It wasn't until they were out in the parking lot by the van, though, that he realized Ginger was coming along, too. "Aren't you going with the rest of them?" he grouched at her.

She shook her head. "No. I'm going with you." She got into the maroon van quickly, before he could object. If God wanted her to be with him this morning or even all day, then she'd go whether she felt like it or not.

As usual, it took a while for Todd to come up the hydraulic lift and for Grandfather to attach the wheelchair to the floor.

After he closed the van's back door and was coming around the outside, Todd said, "I guess you think I'm a chicken for not climbing."

"It's none of my business," Ginger returned.

"You wanted me to go—"

She nodded a little. "Yeah . . . I guess so." She was

glad Grandfather was opening his door, then climbing onto the driver's seat. If there was one thing she didn't want to do, it was to make matters worse.

Grandfather said to her, "I'd like your help choosing a present for the family."

"Sure," she answered. "I did my shopping already." To fill in the silence, she added, "I bought Yosemite picture place mats for Mom and Grant, a tiny toy bear for Lilabet, and a key chain for Joshua. I didn't figure Mattie would need a Yosemite souvenir!"

The van was quiet for a while, then Grandfather asked Todd, "Do you have any shopping to do?"

"No," he replied in a cold voice.

They drove silently through Yosemite Village, then passed the all-too-well-remembered clinic and arrived at the Ahwahnee Hotel. Their visit to its gift shop was just as quiet, and Ginger felt caught up in Todd's suffering.

While Todd chose the slides he wanted, Grandfather decided on a woven Indian basket as a gift for everyone at home. "Think they'd like it?" he asked Ginger.

"It's perfect to put on the family room bookshelves," she said. "Indian things look good with a Spanish house."

"I think so myself," Grandfather said. "I'll buy it."

Before long, they were on their way out of the hotel. They were all pretending nothing had changed since Todd's decision against the "Go for It" climb, but everything was different.

In the parking lot, Grandfather exclaimed, "Oh, no!"

111

Ginger's eyes followed his gaze and saw that her van door wasn't quite shut. "I must have forgotten to lock it!" she wailed and ran for it. What problem had she caused now?

The moment she looked in, she saw it on the floor. "Todd's camera! Someone's returned it!"

"You're kidding!" Grandfather said, then saw it himself.

"You think the boys returned it?" she asked.

They looked around the parking lot, but there was no sign of Kyle or Curt.

"Unless there's a note, I suspect we'll never know who took it or who brought it back," Grandfather replied.

Ginger surveyed the inside of the van. "No note."

Grandfather said, "God has ways of working things out."

"I guess so!" she answered. "I hope it's still okay." She handed the camera to Todd who looked more hopeful than he had in days as he examined it.

"It seems all right," he said. "Even the same number of pictures taken. Let's see if it still works." He turned his wheelchair to take a picture of the Ahwahnee Hotel and Half Dome behind it. As he pressed the button, the camera gave a perfect click. "It sounds fine!"

Ginger's heart swelled with gratefulness. *Thank You, thank You, Lord!* Even if they never learned who'd returned that camera, she knew that Grandfather's kindness to Kyle and Curt had made the difference.

"Hey," she said to Todd, "you look just right with

112

that camera around your neck. Like you're on top of things."

He smiled a little. "I guess so."

"Well," Grandfather said to Todd, "what pictures do you want to take next?"

Todd gave it some thought. "The horseback rides by Happy Isles. My photo session was slightly interrupted."

"Yeah!" Ginger said "By a slide down the hillside."

Todd grinned at her. "So it was."

She returned his grin. "Never let yourself be pushed by a crazy redhead. At least, not till she's learned how."

"Believe me, I won't!" He almost laughed, then rolled his wheelchair toward the back of the van.

By the time they drove off, things seemed a lot better.

They hadn't driven far, though, when Grandfather said, "I . . . I'd better pull off the road. I feel . . . dizzy."

Ginger suddenly recalled something. "Did you take two heart pills at breakfast, Grandfather?"

"By golly, I think I did! Maybe that's it," he said and stopped the van alongside the road.

Ginger eyed him uneasily. "Your face is real white."

He clutched his throat and opened his door. "I'd better get out for a minute. I feel . . . nauseated."

As Grandfather started around the front of the van, she climbed out, too. But he'd no more than got to her side of the van, than he leaned on it. "I feel dizzier yet!"

Todd called out the open van window, "You'd better sit!"

"Maybe . . . I will," Grandfather managed.

His face grew even paler, and he let Ginger help him into her seat. "Here," she said with a gulp, "sit down."

He was no more than in it, than he fell forward, and Ginger made a wild grab for his shoulders.

Todd grabbed Grandfather's shoulders, too, and held them upright against the seat. "Quick! Push his legs in!"

Ginger grabbed Grandfather's limp legs and pushed them into the van. "What are we going to do?" she almost wailed.

They both glanced out for help, but, unbelievable as it seemed, there was no one in sight.

"Pat his cheeks to bring him to!" Todd suggested.

Grandfather's head had fallen forward, and she patted his wrinkled cheeks. "It's not helping at all! *Oh, Lord, help!*"

"Can you buckle him in?" Todd asked. "Pull the seat belt out a long way so you can get it around him."

"What for?" she demanded.

"If he doesn't come to, you're going to have to drive us to the clinic!"

"Me, drive?!" she cried out in disbelief.

"Don't argue! Just buckle him in!"

Frantic, she got the seat belt around Grandfather.

"Okay," Todd said. "Now close the door and come around to the driver's seat."

Ginger shut the van door and raced around to the driver's seat, her stomach churning. "I've never driven! I don't know how!"

"Just get in and close your door! I'll tell you what to

do. First, pull the seat forward."

She felt for the seat lever and jerked the seat forward. Darting a look at Grandfather, hot tears burst to her eyes. "He looks d-dead—"

"He has a pulse in his neck," Todd said, still holding Grandfather upright. "Stop bawling and buckle up!"

Ginger buckled up and, as she wiped her eyes, the words came: "Those who trust in the Lord are like Mount Zion, which can never be shaken, never be moved."

"The engine's already running," Todd said. "All you have to do is drive it a few blocks to the clinic. Now put your right foot by the gas pedal . . . the pedal on the right. On the left is the brake pedal."

Ginger looked down at the pedals and her sandaled feet.

"Okay, now, shift to D with the gearshift."

Carefully, she moved the gearshift to D.

"Good. Now, pull the emergency brake." He pointed.

Ginger pulled it and the van moved. "Yii!"

She grabbed the steering wheel, then took another look at Grandfather and knew she'd do anything to save his life.

"Now step on the gas pedal just a little."

She stepped on it and the van jerked forward.

"Just a little! Do everything just a little."

She tried again, not so hard, and the van moved slowly forward. *Those who trust in the Lord are like Mount Zion, which can never be shaken. . . .*

"Now turn the steering wheel toward the road,"

Todd said, his voice level.

Her foot still on the gas pedal, she turned the steering wheel, and the van bounced jerkily up onto the road.

"Turn right!" Todd yelled.

She turned the steering wheel, her palms sweating.

"Not so much!"

She wheeled the van back in time to keep them on the road.

"Steady now . . . steady . . ." Todd said.

Gripping the steering wheel, she peered out over the van's hood. She was driving . . . really driving! The van zigzagged a bit, but there were no other cars. "Those who trust in the Lord . . ." she said aloud and was glad she'd watched Grandfather drive on the way here.

"Keep going . . . steady," Todd said. "In a few minutes, we'll be at the clinic driveway. You'll have to turn slowly when you turn in. I'll tell you when."

She wondered how he knew so much about driving, but this was no time to ask. Besides, it was hard to keep the van from weaving all over the road. "Those who trust in the Lord are like Mount Zion, which can never be shaken—"

After what felt like a long time, Todd said, "Okay, there's the clinic driveway. When we get to it, just turn the wheel a little."

Ginger waited until they were almost to the driveway, then turned the wheel slowly. Amazingly, the van turned in.

"Quick, turn the wheel back!"

She whipped it back. A green truck dodged past, missing them by inches, and the driver honked angrily.

"When we get to the emergency door, we have to stop," Todd warned uneasily. "Remember the brake is your left pedal. Take your foot off the gas and push down on the brake."

She pushed down hard, and the van squealed to a stop, then spurted forward again.

"Foot off the gas!" Todd yelled, so she just lifted both feet and the van rolled slowly but surely into a tree, hitting with a soft bump.

"Uff!" Todd said. "Now move the gearshift to P and honk the horn for all you're worth!"

She did both, honking the horn wildly, for Grandfather looked limp as a rag doll.

Seconds later, people ran from the clinic.

"Hurry!" Ginger yelled out the window, tears bursting to her eyes again. "My grandfather's awfully sick!"

They stared at her in amazement, then ran to Grandfather.

God, please don't let him die! she prayed.

In moments, a man was taking Grandfather's pulse, then ordering a stretcher. "What happened?" he asked.

"I think he took two of his heart pills!" Ginger said. "They're in the blue plastic pillbox in his shirt pocket."

Moments later, Grandfather was being carried into the clinic on a stretcher and someone was turning off the ignition for her, then helping Todd unattach his

117

wheelchair from the floor of the van.

"You did all right, Ginger," Todd said as he came down the hydraulic lift in his wheelchair. "You did all right!"

In the clinic waiting room, a lady phoned for the rangers to find Aunt Jennie, Uncle Charlie, and Berkie.

Ginger sat down on a chair. "Pray for Grandfather."

"I have been," Todd replied, his blue-green eyes meeting hers with seriousness.

It seemed forever before a ranger brought Aunt Jennie, Uncle Charlie, and Berkie to the waiting room. "What happened?" they asked, wild with concern.

"Grandfather got dizzy—" Tears burst to Ginger's eyes.

"He passed out," Todd finished for her. "The doctor is looking at him now. Ginger had to drive the van here."

"*Ginger drove the van?!*" Aunt Jennie exclaimed.

"Ginger drove?" Uncle Charlie and Berkie echoed.

"Todd told me how," Ginger said. "Grandfather looked like he was dying!"

"Please sit down," the lady in charge said. "The doctor will be out to talk with you as soon as possible."

Todd explained everything again, even about the camera being returned to the van.

Aunt Jennie shook her head and looked at Ginger. "I don't know how you drove. I'm so grateful you two are all right."

Berkie bit her lips together, then said, "Me, too!"

Uncle Charlie said, "Make that three of us!"

Not too much later, the doctor stepped into the waiting room. "Mr. Gabriel will be fine. He'll be out in a minute. A good thing you young people got him here."

As Ginger looked at Todd, his square chin wobbled, then tears filled both pairs of eyes. She jumped from her chair and threw her arms around him, wheelchair and all. "We did it! We did it! Thank You, God!"

Todd hugged her back hard, barely choking off a sob.

Just then, Grandfather walked into the waiting room. "Hey, what's all of this about?" he asked.

Everyone stared at him. His color had returned, and he looked like he'd be all right.

"Oh, I'm so glad!" Ginger said and ran to give him a relieved hug.

From behind her she heard Todd say in a firm voice, "I've changed my mind. I'm going on the 'Go for It' climb."

Ginger turned to him in amazement. "You are?"

Todd nodded. "I am. If I can depend on you driving the van, I can depend on others pulling and pushing my wheelchair when I need help. I can trust in the Lord that much, too."

"I'm so glad!" Ginger returned. "I'm so glad!" She beamed at him and realized that she loved him. In the midst of everything the Lord had given her love for Todd.

She told the others, "God reminded me of the verse on the church program yesterday, 'Those who trust in the Lord are like Mount Zion, which can never be shaken, never be moved.' "

All of them—Berkie, Aunt Jennie, Uncle Charlie, and Grandfather—smiled shakily at them. Then Grandfather came over and put a hand on Todd's shoulder. "You two have given us a living sermon about trusting God. All I can say is a hearty 'Amen'!"

Ginger's heart overflowed with joy. Not only was Grandfather fine, but Todd was going to climb a mountain. Probably it wouldn't be easy, but he was going for it . . . really going for it.

Thank You! Ginger prayed. *Oh, thank You, Lord!*

For information about the "Go for It!" Adventure, contact:

Summit Adventure
P. O. Box 498
Bass Lake, CA 93604

209-642-3899
1-800-827-1282

HERE COMES GINGER!

God, stop Mom's wedding!

Ginger's world is falling apart. Her mom has recently become a Christian and, even worse, has fallen in love with Grant Gabriel. Ginger can't stand the thought of leaving their little house near the beach . . . moving in with Grant and his two children . . . trading in her "brown cave of a bedroom" for a yellow canopied bed.

Ginger tries to fight the changes she knows are coming—green fingernails, salt in the sugar bowl, a near disaster at the beach. But she finds that change can happen inside her, too, when she meets the Lord her mom has come to trust.

The Ginger Series
    Here Comes Ginger!   A Job for an Angel
    Off to a New Start   Absolutely Green

  ELAINE L. SCHULTE is a southern Californian, like Ginger. She has written many stories, articles, and books for all ages, but the **Ginger Trumbell Books** is her first series for kids.

Chariot Books™
David C. Cook Publishing Co.

OFF TO A NEW START

Aoooouuuuh!
Aooooouuuuuh!

The blast of Ginger's conch shell sounds through the Gabriels' house. But is it a call to battle or a plea for peace?

Some days Ginger isn't sure, as she struggles to find her place in her new "combined" family, in her new school, and as a new child of God. With the wise counsel of Grandfather Gabriel and the support of her family, Ginger learns some important lessons about making friends and making peace.

The Ginger Series

Here Comes Ginger!   A Job for an Angel
Off to a New Start   Absolutely Green

ELAINE L. SCHULTE is a southern Californian, like Ginger. She has written many stories, articles, and books for all ages, but the **Ginger Trumbell Books** is her first series for kids.

Chariot Books™
David C. Cook Publishing Co.

A JOB FOR AN ANGEL

Love your neighbor?

October brings two new people into Ginger's life—and they couldn't be more different from each other.

Ginger looks forward to her Wednesday afternoon job of "baby-sitting" Aunt Alice. She may be elderly and ill, but she's cheerful and fun to be with. At school, however, Ginger is stuck trying to befriend grouchy Robin Lindberg, who never misses an opportunity to be nasty.

Ginger knows that "love your neighbor" includes the Robins as well as the Aunt Alices . . . but knowing doesn't make it easy. . . .

The Ginger Series
Here Comes Ginger!   A Job for an Angel
Off to a New Start   Absolutely Green

ELAINE L. SCHULTE is a southern Californian, like Ginger. She has written many stories, articles, and books for all ages, but the **Ginger Trumbell Books** is her first series for kids.

Chariot Books™
David C. Cook Publishing Co.

ABSOLUTELY GREEN

Green with envy— that's Ginger!

Life with her new "combined family" has just begun to feel natural when Ginger's mom and stepdad make an announcement: a new baby is on the way!

They sure are happy about it, but Ginger doesn't know what to think. It's clear that her stepbrother, Joshua, is anything but pleased—and for some reason, the news seems to make him grouchier than ever with Ginger.

Together Ginger's family discovers how God's love can conquer even feelings of resentment and jealousy.

The Ginger Series
Here Comes Ginger!　　A Job for an Angel
Off to a New Start　　Absolutely Green

ELAINE L. SCHULTE is a southern Californian, like Ginger. She has written many stories, articles, and books for all ages, but the **Ginger Trumbell Books** is her first series for kids.

Chariot Books™
David C. Cook Publishing Co.

ONLY KIDDING, VICTORIA

You've got to be kidding!

Spend the summer at a resort lodge in Minnesota . . . with her *family?* When she's been looking forward to endless days of good times with her new friends from school?

Victoria can't believe her parents are serious, but nothing she can do or say will change their minds. It's off to Little Raccoon Lake, a nowhere place where she's sure there will be nothing to do.

But the summer holds a lot of surprises—like Nina, one year older and a whole lot tougher, who scoffs at rules . . . and at Vic for bothering to keep them. And the bittersweet pang that comes with each letter from her best friend, Chelsie, reminding Vic of what she's missing back home. But the biggest surprise is Victoria's discovery of some things that have been right under her nose all along . . . .

Don't miss any books in The Victoria Mahoney Series!

#1 Just Victoria
#2 More Victoria
#3 Take a Bow, Victoria

#4 Only Kidding, Victoria
#5 Maybe It's Love, Victoria
#6 Autograph, Please, Victoria

SHELLY NIELSEN lives in Minneapolis, Minnesota, with her husband and two Yorkshire terriers.

AUTOGRAPH PLEASE, VICTORIA

Vickie Mahoney, celebrity?

The weeks before Christmas are exciting ones for Victoria. Winning a national contest brings attention from teachers, an interview on local TV, and a new excuse for best friend, Chelsie, to dream and scheme on Vic's behalf ("Do you want to hear my Vic Mahoney Promotion Plan?").

But Vic is distracted from her stardom by her little brother's big troubles. Matthew's "adjustment problems" in first grade turn out to be a learning disability. Once again the Mahoney family is put to the test, and once again their faith in God, affection for each other, and slightly crazy sense of humor help them survive.

In the process, Vic realizes a little more about who she is and what really matters.

Don't miss any books in
The Victoria Mahoney Series!

SHELLY NIELSEN lives in Minneapolis, Minnesota, with her husband and two Yorkshire terriers.